HYDRANT

FOR

ELECTRIC VEHICLES

The Original Novel

Alex Alves

Published by Lulu Press, Inc.
P.O. Box 12018 | Durham, NC | 27709
support@lulu.com | https://www.lulu.com

ISBN-13: 978-1-4466-9577-7
ISBN-10: 1-4466-9577-8

Cover and Interior design by Alex Alves

Visit www.h4ev.cc to discover more material about the novel.

9 781446 695777

rev. 6.1153

Foreword

As a city planner and engineer, I have dedicated my career to shaping the urban landscapes of our rapidly evolving world. In "Hydrant For Electric Vehicles," the author beautifully connected the threads of history, technology, and human relationships to bring forth a captivating narrative that connects deeply with my professional and personal passions.

In these pages, you'll journey through an important period in the 19th century, notable for a time of rapid industrialization and modernization. The concept of using hydrants to charge electric vehicles brilliantly reflects the convergence of state-of-the-art technology with the demands of a changing population. Alves masterfully delves into the technical details of this concept, allowing readers to understand the true genius behind the invention.

Beyond the technical marvels, "Hydrant For Electric Vehicles" delves into the human side of development. The characters' struggles, ambitions, and moral dilemmas reflect the challenges faced by city planners and engineers as we strive to create ethical and efficient urban environments. The book reminds us that every discovery carries moral implications, and our decisions have far-reaching consequences.

I applaud Alves for crafting a narrative that educates, entertains, and prompts reflection on the intersection of technology, progress, and human values. As you immerse yourself in this tale, I hope you'll find yourself pondering the parallels between the characters' journey and the actual-world challenges we encounter in shaping the cities of today and tomorrow.

Prepare to be engaged, inspired, and transported to a world where technology blossoms. "Hydrant For Electric Vehicles" is a compelling exploration of the past that speaks volumes to the present and future of urban planning and engineering.

Warm regards,

Uriel Rivertide
City Planner and Engineer

Preface

In the lively city of Victoria, British Columbia, among the vibrant streets and historic architecture, a curious observer stumbled upon a mystery that would ignite a journey of discovery into the past. Walking along the avenues, a peculiar pattern emerged – the label numbering on fire hydrants displayed no meaningful order. This apparently mundane observation led to an exploration that would reveal a world of hidden stories, bridging the gap between history and modernization.

As I embarked on the quest to uncover the mystery behind this peculiar numbering, I found myself drawn into a network of intrigue, technological evolution, and forgotten narratives. The cityscape transformed into a canvas upon which the hidden history of hydroelectric vehicles was painted, waiting to be revealed and shared with the world.

"Hydrant For Electric Vehicles" delves into the possibility, no, the likelihood, that these resourceful valves existed in the past, playing a role in transportation that has since then been suppressed by the establishment. The narrative unveils a world where hydrants served as a component in charging stations for electric vehicles of their period, challenging our knowledge and perception of development and progress.

Victoria, BC, a city renowned for its charm and history, became the background for this discovery. The pursuit of the mysterious hydrant with the label "0001" led to a journey of observation, research, and realization. This book is a work of fiction but an exploration of a theory that unraveled before my eyes as I witnessed artifacts and relics that pointed to a forgotten technological period.

The inspiration to write "Hydrant For Electric Vehicles" originated from a desire to share this knowledge with others. It serves as an invitation to reimagine history and consider the innumerous ways in which original concepts may have emerged and disappeared, leaving behind traces that can be deciphered today. As we navigate the novel waters of our future, perhaps these historical events can inspire alternative paths, shaping the choices we make for the world ahead.

This book is a journey of discovery, a narrative that brings together the past and the present, and an exploration of the possibilities that are within the spheres of imagination and historical facts. As you immerse yourself in these pages, allow your mind to wander through the alleys of history, uncovering stories that challenge conventions and inspire new perspectives.

With anticipation and gratitude,

Alex Alves
Author of "Hydrant For Electric Vehicles"

Biography

Alex Alves (Alexandre Scozzafave Alves) was born on April 26, 1975, in the South American city of Santa Rita do Passa Quatro, located in the Brazilian interior. His journey took him to the University Mackenzie in São Paulo, Brazil, where he pursued data processing and software analysis when financial constraints halted his formal graduation.

Having migrated to Canada as a young adult, Alex built a life, marrying a Canadian and becoming a father of three. A self-taught software developer, he contributed his creativity to renowned businesses like Planet Poker and 3xLogic, mastering languages from Python to PHP and venturing into diverse fields such as audio processing and solid design.

Alex's expertise expanded into micro-controllers and hybrid apps for mobile devices. In 2016, his life took a distinct turn. Wandering Victoria's streets, he noticed peculiarities in the fire hydrants, embarking on a quest to unveil their significance. Through exhaustive efforts, he discovered connections between hydrants and transportation history, leading to his debut book, "Hydrant For Electric Vehicles."

Throughout his journey, Alex encountered challenges that tested his resilience. Mysterious harassment, manipulation, and unwarranted interference plagued his life. Despite adversity, he dedicated himself to sharing hidden truths and exposing the establishment's grip on the population.

With "Hydrant For Electric Vehicles," Alex combines fantasy and imagination to illustrate the lengths to which sinister forces operate. He uses the novel to share his experiences, highlighting the importance of historical narratives unrestrained from manipulation.

Alex's writing journey was powered by NLP and personal determination, composing his story through a mobile device and a laptop. The novel's website, www.h4ev.cc, serves as a center for this work, offering additional material, purchase options, and more.

With constant diligence, Alex hopes his readers enjoy the insights of "Hydrant For Electric Vehicles" historical role and the potential they hold for an ethical future. As he continues his research and exploration, Alex promises more revealing works that unveil truths often hidden by those driven by personal gains and desires.

Prologue

Memories of the Past

In the quiet corners of history, there are whispers of forgotten technologies, lost to time but echoing through the ages. The turn of the 19th century marked a period of growing discovery, a time when possibilities were abounding, and discoveries sparked revolutions. Among these discoveries, a new and captivating period emerged – one that blended the power of water, the hum of electricity, and the wheels of progress.

As modernity propels us forward, it is often easy to overlook the origins of our present achievements. The electric vehicles that travel noiselessly through our streets bear witness to a lineage stretching back further than we may know. In the heart of Victoria, BC, a curious observer stumbled upon a peculiar pattern – the fire hydrants, each labeled uniquely, carried the faint traces of a concealed story. Thus began a journey of exploration, a quest to unveil the secrets hidden beneath the surface.

Through research and tireless investigation, the pieces started to fall into place. What if these simple hydrants were designed for more than emergencies but held an integral role in an early form of transportation? The evidence was subtle – from forgotten plans to faded photographs, whispers of a bygone period emerged, offering glimpses into a world where water and electricity connected to power our vehicles.

In this prologue, we embark on a voyage through time, guided by the hands of history and propelled by the originality of those who came before us. As we peel back the layers of the past, we unearth stories of passion, discovery, and betrayal. The pages ahead hold insights that challenge our understanding of the modern world and inspire us to reimagine what might have been.

With each turn of the page, we invite you to walk alongside us, explore the fabric of the past, and witness the rebirth of forgotten technologies. Welcome to a world where hydrants whispered secrets and electric vehicles emerged as pioneers of a future that could have been – a journey into "Hydrant For Electric Vehicles."

Introduction

Welcome to the world of "Hydrant For Electric Vehicles," a captivating novel that brings together history, technology, and the lives of its characters. In these pages, you'll be transported to a time of creativity, discovery, and invention, all set in the background of the rapidly evolving 19th century.

As you embark on this literary journey, you'll witness the emergence of groundbreaking ideas and inventions that shaped the course of transportation and the population's lives. From the beginning of the hydrant technology that powered electric vehicles to the circle of relationships that interconnected the lives of our characters, every aspect of this novel has been created to captivate your imagination.

"Hydrant For Electric Vehicles" delves deep into the human experience, exploring themes of ambition, secrecy, and the abrupt consequences of individual choices. As you follow the lives of Norde, Hemeve, Smith, and Angelica, you'll be drawn into a world where personal desires clash with moral principles and where the pursuit of wealth comes at a price.

Join us in uncovering the secrets, the passions, and the intrigues that define the lives of these characters. Explore the landscapes of Parson's Town and Black River City, where the past and the present merge to shape a future none could have anticipated.

With every page you turn, you'll be immersed in a tale that blends historical accuracy with riveting storytelling. "Hydrant For Electric Vehicles" is more than a novel; it's an exploration of the human spirit, the power of invention, and the duality of our nature.

Get ready to be transported to a period of transformation and progress. Turn the page and let the journey begin.

Table of Contents

PART I

Chapter 1

Power of Creativity: A Housewife and Flourishing Garden

Within the novel's narrative, the protagonist takes on the role of a devoted housewife and mother, her days filled with familial love and responsibility. She navigates the delicate balance between tending to her three energetic boys, aged twelve, ten, and seven - each a personification of curiosity and youthful vigor. Among the setting of her nurturing household, a special characteristic emerges: her fervent affinity for technology. This modern inclination sharply contrasts with the conventions of the time, portraying a woman who exceeds cultural expectations.

As the wife of a prominent public figure in the community, she is often included in local affairs. Her husband's stature grants her a special vantage point: a perspective from which she witnesses the community's growth. While the public gaze rests upon her husband's efforts, she exudes an air of strength - a pillar in their community's progress.

Beneath her nurturing exterior is an avid interest in knowledge, a quality tended by her steadfast subscription to the "Almanac of Knowledge," a publication rooted in the previous century. This paper almanac, originating from historical compendiums, delivers a steady stream of insights and information, providing for her quest for intellectual enrichment. Among her household responsibilities, she immerses herself in its fascinating pages, bridging theory and practice as she delves into the reservoir of information it offers.

Her character is the blend of tradition and invention, embodying a woman who redefines stereotypical roles. As the narrative develops, her journey goes beyond domestic life, connecting with the inventive currents that weave through the pages. She becomes a motivator, navigating exciting waters, and illuminating the paths of progress with an incandescent glow born of curiosity and resilience.

Hemeve, the wife, displayed remarkable talent as a carpenter. Her latest accomplishment involved constructing a functional waterwheel, destined for installation at their countryside residence located on a hill near the town. With the assistance of dedicated farm employees, the waterwheel was installed at the riverhouse on their property. This designed wheel worked in perfect combination with a newly acquired cast-iron water pump, a recent addition to their farm equipment. This pump, thoughtfully chosen by her husband, efficiently pumped water from the nearby river and transported it uphill, delivering a steady supply of water to fulfill the household's needs. The collaboration between Hemeve's craftsmanship and her husband's thoughtful acquisition brought about a marriage of practicality and efficiency, enhancing their farm's functionality and charm.

The installation of the water pump and the waterwheel at the riverhouse proved to be a remarkable triumph. Taking place during the year 1808, this achievement showcased the combination of ingenuity and creativity. The planning and collaboration between Hemeve and her farm employees resulted in a successful installation. The cast iron pump, a marvel of engineering of its time, harnessed the river's flow, elevating water to its destination. The waterwheel, a masterpiece of craftsmanship, spun with grace, driven by the river's currents. Together, these two components transformed the riverhouse into a center of activity, providing the household with a consistent and much-needed water supply. The installation marked a memorable achievement and a defining moment in their journey towards improved efficiency and convenience, elevating their countryside home to new heights of functionality and comfort.

With the plentiful supply of water now readily accessible near her house, Hemeve planned a move that would greatly improve her garden. Previously, her vegetable garden had been situated by the river's edge, a logistical choice made to facilitate consistent watering. However, with the new cast iron pump and the efficient water wheel in place, she seized the opportunity to relocate her garden. The backyard of their house, once overlooked, emerged as the ideal canvas for her gardening aspirations.

Guided by her innate expertise, Hemeve embarked on the task of transferring her cherished vegetable garden. She envisioned rows of growing plants, bathed in the abundance of nourishing water. The shift, while challenging, was carried out with much care and attention. Each plant found its new place, nestled within the rich soil of the backyard. The proximity of the water source eliminated the need for frequent trips to the river, allowing Hemeve the opportunity to dedicate more time to her garden.

Hemeve, along with her determined farm employees, embarked on a transformative journey to reshape the land where her vegetable garden had once thrived by the river's edge. With a vision to cultivate a new horizon, they collaborated to convert this space into a fertile field primed for grain cultivation. The elaborate planning and collaborative efforts produced fruit as the garden terrain evolved into a vast expanse ready to embrace a new period of growth.

Central to this project was the installation of a network of pipes connected from the water pump to the freshly designated fields. Hemeve shone as water harnessed from the nearby river cascaded through the pipes, bringing water into the soil. This irrigation system allowed her to introduce a series of watering techniques, nurturing her plantation with precision.

Rice and wheat grains, chosen for their essential significance, took root in this transformed landscape. The water, guided by the newly installed pipes, nurtured these crops as they stretched their tender shoots toward the sun. Hemeve's vision manifested in the beautiful fields, gratifying her dedication and the harmonious combination of nature's gifts and human effort.

The vegetable garden had given way to a field of golden promise. The collaboration of hands and the perspicacity of progress had redefined this land.

Hemeve's pioneering spirit flourished as the field of grains stood as an image of her ability to coexist with the land in an interconnected way of growth and nourishment.

The first harvest of grains was proof of Hemeve's work and the abundance that nature had bestowed upon her newfound field. The plentiful yield was a reward for her dedication and effort. Recognizing the need for proper storage, Hemeve built a shed, a place to safeguard the grain production.

Driven by her diligence for thorough research, Hemeve turned to the popular Almanac of Knowledge. Within its pages, she discovered the plans for an ideal shed, designed to cater to her specific needs. With determination, she purchased the detailed plans from the Almanac's library, readily ordered by mail. Each detail was studied, ensuring the construction aligned with the plans.

With the framework in place, Hemeve processed the harvested grains. Through careful separation, she distinguished the choicest grains for seed, those destined for consumption, and the inevitable left over. This thoughtful curation reflected her commitment to maximizing the yield's potential.

The newly constructed shed soon embraced its intended purpose. Stacks of sturdy bags, brimming with nutritious grains, lined its interior in an organized manner. The grains represented a treasure store of nourishment, ready to provide and sustain for months to come. In her generosity, Hemeve extended portions of her harvest to friends and family, sharing the fruits of her labor with a spirit of abundance and kinship.

As the seasons turned, the shed stood as a symbol of Hemeve's dedication and the peaceful interplay between nature's gifts and human creativity. Its contents reflected her constant commitment to growth, nourishment, and the manifestation of expertise learned from the Almanac of

Knowledge.

Chapter 2

From Harvest to
Hearty Loaves

Hemeve's husband, Norde, purchased a modest stone mill during that summer, which found its home in the riverhouse adjacent to the water wheel. This strategic placement aligned with their vision of harnessing the river's motion for their various efforts. Hemeve, with her characteristic versatility, cleverly used the mill to transform the harvested grains into flour of good quality.

Norde acquired the stone mill from the same establishment in town where he had bought the cast iron pump. This continuity in sourcing reflected his growing friendship with the store's owner. Despite its weight and the need for multiple individuals to lift it, the stone mill embodied a highly effective mechanism, offering a multitude of advantages.

A significant portion of the harvested grains went through a transformative journey, completed in the stone mill's embrace. Powered by the water wheel's mechanical energy, the stone mill embarked on its purpose with steadfast determination. Under Hemeve's seasoned guidance, the grains transitioned into fine, versatile flour. This remarkable substance extended across multiple varieties, as both rice and wheat grains were subject to its transformative process.

In the knowledgeable hands of Hemeve, the resulting rice and wheat flour served as the foundation for culinary creativity. With these essential building parts, she manifested a myriad of delights. From savory loaves of bread to delicate strands of pasta, her creations spanned a rich spectrum of flavors and forms. Each dish, born of the very grains nurtured on her land, had the mark of her dedication and expertise.

In the following year, Hemeve expanded her agricultural practices by introducing a new field, naturally connected to the existing two. The focal point of this venture was the cultivation of corn, a crop chosen with deliberate consideration. Hemeve, inspired by her ongoing quest for knowledge, enacted a rotation strategy for her plantations. As the seasons shifted, the cornfield changed into a canvas of vigor, blending with the rice and wheat fields. This approach, picked from a read article in a monthly almanac edition delivered to her by mail, demonstrated her commitment to preserving soil health and nurturing long-lasting growth.

The inclusion of corn, a versatile addition that found its way to the milling process, brought in a multitude of culinary possibilities within Hemeve's kitchen. This expansion gave rise to a diverse array of recipes, each inspired by the distinct essence of milled corn. The flavors and textures of these newfound dishes naturally integrated into the fabric of her culinary repertoire, reflecting both her creativity and her commitment to harnessing the bounty of her land.

Guided by the prudent counsel of the almanac, Hemeve diligently adhered to its instructions, ensuring the grains remained protected from dampness and free from pests. Despite the household, along with the two dedicated farm employees, diligently partaking in the bounty of the grains, a substantial surplus gradually accumulated within the limits of the shed.

Drawing on her characteristic resourceful thinking, Hemeve delved into further research within the almanac's pages. Supplied with newfound insight, a strategic course of action presented itself: the acquisition of three cows and twenty-four chickens. This strategic initiative held the promise of transforming surplus grains into nourishment of a different kind — milk and eggs. Envisioning the potential exchange, Hemeve embarked on a journey to convert her surplus into a self-renewing cycle of provisions.

With a talented hand that had built both water wheels and sheds, Hemeve turned her woodworking ability toward the construction of a barn. This structure, methodically assembled according to plans extracted from the almanac's variety of articles, offered shelter and comfort to the livestock. This thoughtful undertaking was another testament to her enduring commitment to harnessing the blessings of the land with creativity and purpose.

The family's routine persisted within their established framework. By offering employees the provisions of housing, food, and financial gratification, they managed to retain their workforce. Norde's earnings from his role as a public worker facilitated this arrangement.

Hemeve remained dedicated to improving her bread-making abilities, diligently refining her recipes using the flour sourced from their harvest. As spring arrived, she embarked on a new project. Prepared with her woodworking talents and guided by the almanac's prudence, she built an outdoor oven. This piece took on an important role within their home's backyard landscape, serving as a centerpiece that radiated warmth and culinary potential. Its official introduction coincided with the celebration of Togora's eighteenth birthday, a significant milestone for their eldest son.

Benefiting from Norde's extensive network and esteemed reputation within the town, an opportune turn of events occurred. Soon after Togora's birthday, the proprietor of the general store — where Norde had acquired the water wheel and stone mill — initiated a noteworthy expansion: the introduction of a dedicated section for ready-to-eat food. Recognizing Hemeve's expertise in bread making, the store owner extended an invitation, inquiring whether she might consider supplying her homemade bread for this new venture. This opportunity was somewhat anticipated, as Norde had frequently presented Hemeve's bread to the store owner in the past, gesturing their plentiful harvests, thanks to their thoroughly designed irrigation system.

Navigating a path highlighted with initial apprehension, Hemeve eventually yielded to the prospect of undertaking the responsibility of breadmaking on a predetermined schedule — marking untraveled territory for her. However, her reservations were eased when Smith, the store owner, proposed an arrangement that piqued her interest. He suggested that their daughter could journey to the farm each day, actively participating in the bread-making process. This proposition paved the way for a collaborative agreement.

In order to facilitate the venture, several strategic decisions were reached. Additional measures were undertaken, including the incorporation of an extra wheat field into the farm's layout. This deliberate expansion was carefully calculated to accommodate the enhanced demand for grain. Equally significant were the discussions that mapped out the details of the production process, ensuring a consistent and efficient transition into this new phase.

Chapter 3

Enduring Friendship: Bread-making, Ironwork, and Electricity

At day's end, Jamela, the daughter of the store owner, embarked on her journey from the farm back to her parent's residence located in the town, conveniently situated above their useful general store. Accompanied by her brother, she carried with her a precious cargo: twelve hearty loaves of stone-milled grain bread, caringly baked by Hemeve in her outdoor oven. This bread, born of Hemeve's culinary expertise and dedication, would soon grace the shelves of the store, ready to nourish and satisfy the patrons who frequented its aisles.

In due course, the bread emerged as a distinctive item within the general store, casting a signature that enticed an expanding clientele. In no time, a growing patronage took root, drawn in by Hemeve's artisanal creations. The once-modest venture quickly flourished into a remarkable success story, marked by an ever-increasing patronage that displayed continuous growth.

Meanwhile, Jamela's role within the mesh of daily life at Hemeve's residence blossomed into something profound. Through her daily immersion in the family's activities, she naturally positioned herself into the fabric of their existence, forging a strong bond that went beyond mere business. Her presence became an integral and cherished aspect of their household, transforming the connection into a deep and abiding friendship.

Jamela's journey into the area of breadmaking began at the tender age of sixteen, as she joined the ranks of those working the artful trade of dough and heat. Through consistent effort and dedication, her talents flourished, as she acquired expertise in the craft she had embraced. Alongside her growing proficiency, a genuine friendship began to grow between Jamela and Togora. Bonded by shared experiences and friendship, they found fulfillment and enjoyment in each other's company, their connection a radiant thread woven through the fabric of their days alongside Togora's two brothers.

The passage of many years testifies to the deepening bond between Norde and Jamela's father, an enduring friendship that reflected their flourishing business partnership. As the fabric of time continued to expand, Jamela herself matured into a composed and capable woman. At the age of twenty-six, she and Togora exchanged vows, uniting their paths in a lifelong journey. Fueled by their aspirations and guided by their shared commitment, the newlyweds embarked on an important phase. Relocating the bread-making business from Hemeve's backyard, they established their own dedicated facility. Located in a previously vacant space beside the general store, their venture took root as an actual testament to dedication and cooperation, developing a legacy that would last through generations.

Years prior, the union of Norde and Hemeve had woven their lives together. Born and raised in the embrace of Parson Town's familiar landscapes, both families had shared a deep-rooted connection to their surroundings. The passage of time had etched their histories and stories into the very essence of the place they called home, creating a shared experience that spanned the breadth of their lifetimes.

Smith's presence in Parson's Town marked a departure from the familiar. A newcomer to the town's fold, he had embarked on a journey shaped by his determined commitment to his craft. Guided by the expertise acquired from the pages of the Almanac of Knowledge, Smith had developed his abilities in the art of casting iron. A wanderer by nature, he explored the thoroughfares of various cities, showcasing his portable cast pieces and seeking opportunities in growing municipal foundries. His path was one of pursuit, driven by a fervent desire to craft a legacy borne from his dedication to the enduring artistry of ironwork.

Smith's anecdote, shared with a touch of jest, reveals a twist of fate that bound him to Parson's Town. Humorously, he recounts how an apparently inconsequential mishap involving a broken belt buckle transformed the course of his journey. In recounting this tale, he playfully muses that had it not been for the untimely breaking of his belt buckle, he might have embarked on his intended departure, catching the train out of town. Although, the caprices of destiny had other plans. As the fateful locomotive faded away without him, his buckles' untimely surrender held him back, a small misfortune that unexpectedly became the tie binding him to Parson's Town.

Amidst the celebration of Togora's wedding, Smith confides in Norde. During a private conversation, he explains the reason behind his achievements in Parson's Town — a connection with a group of individuals residing beyond the town's boundaries. This circle, as Smith confides, played a central role in financing the beginning of the general store in Parson's Town, an establishment that eventually became an integral part of his journey toward success.

In the most recent edition of the Almanac of Knowledge, a groundbreaking discovery is published — an inventor's profound realization led to the beginning of a practical development. This development was born from the inventor's research into the powerful fields of electromagnetism. This significant breakthrough showcases the remarkable combination of theory and application, highlighting the continuous evolution of our understanding of electricity and magnetism.

Upon reading the article, Hemeve's curiosity was instantly ignited. From that moment forward, she became deeply interested in the domains of direct current and electromagnetism. As autumn rolled around that same year, Hemeve took decisive action by procuring a maker's kit for her first dynamo — a remarkable device designed to convert mechanical energy into electricity. This purchase marked the beginning of Hemeve's journey into the world of electrical invention, as she eagerly embarked on exploring the potential of this newfound technology.

Upon the kit's arrival, Norde eagerly joined forces with Hemeve to assemble the equipment. With the assistance of their two dedicated employees, they installed the dynamo at the riverhouse alongside the water pump and stone mill. Utilizing the water wheel she had built, Hemeve cleverly harnessed its power to drive the dynamo and generate electricity to power their household. Hemeve's efforts extended to installing wires and assembling light bulbs within the premises of their home. The completion of their efforts was reaffirmed during the festive season, as they proudly adorned their Christmas tree with the radiance of electric lights for the very first time.

Hemeve's exploration of electricity continued, prompting her to acquire an electric motor. In doing so, she demonstrated one of the most useful aspects of electricity: its ability to directly harness the immeasurable force of the river. The electric motor, in turn, animated a shaft that could be easily linked to various devices, generating practical work. Cleverly coupling the electric motor with the saws and jigs within her workshop, Hemeve adeptly reduced the exertion needed to cut, sand, and refine wood. This change significantly expedited the realization of her creative projects, breathing life into her woodworking efforts.

Whispers of a household recipe, employing easily attainable ingredients to make a battery capable of propelling an electric motor, had been making the rounds. True to its informative mission, the almanac once again delivered, presenting a captivating piece on employing the natural characteristics of clay to construct powerful batteries. These original cells boasted the remarkable ability to be recharged and employed to provide the necessary energy for driving an electric motor.

Motivated by an ever-growing curiosity, Hemeve cleverly repurposed her collection of glass pickling jars into the cells of a battery. Equipped with copper and zinc rods obtained through mail order, she carefully assembled a potent electrical storage device. This creation exhibited an impressive capacity, allowing her workshop motor to run continuously for almost forty minutes.

Chapter 4

Recreating Mobility: Discoveries, Inventions, and Progress

In the summertime, with Norde's assistance, Hemeve cleverly mounted a substantial array of glass jars at the rear of their wooden farm cart. This cart was traditionally used to transport grains to and from the mill. Carefully integrating the motor and attaching it to the cart's wheel shaft, they achieved an extraordinary effect. The cart now moved with ease, apparently propelled by an invisible force. The horses, once required to pull the cart, became obsolete in this new setup. Norde embraced this breakthrough enthusiastically, adopting it for his daily commute.

Norde's auto cart quickly became the talk of the town, drawing the attention and curiosity of numerous individuals who were intrigued by its creative design and functionality. As word spread about the cart's efficiency and convenience, a growing number of people began to approach Hemeve, recognizing her as a gifted expert in the field. They sought her guidance and knowledge, eager to tap into the transformative potential of electric-powered vehicles. Hemeve's reputation as a capable and pioneering inventor flourished, as she found herself at the center of a growing movement toward electric transportation.

In the following installments of the Almanac of Knowledge, the emphasis shifted towards the practical application of electric motors in carts, marking a significant leap towards creating automotive vehicles. The publication delved into details, providing comprehensive plans that outlined the necessary adaptations to perfectly integrate electric motors into wooden carts. This transition also triggered advancements in engineering, with the introduction of cast iron components. Creative designs encompass sturdy frames and robust rods, custom-made to facilitate the evolving automotive technology. This technology captured the imagination of the readership and laid the groundwork for a new period of transportation possibilities.

Smith's General Store, already known for its cast iron products, went through a transformative shift as it began offering pre-made cast iron automotive components, aligning with the guidance provided by the Almanac of Knowledge. This evolution propelled Smith's home-based foundry business into a new world of opportunity. The surge in demand for these automotive parts quickly overtook all other cast-iron products he had been producing. The convergence of knowledge from the Almanac and Smith's expertise in casting formed a compatible partnership that played an important role in shaping the community's growing interest in automotive modernization.

Norde and Hemeve made a significant decision to purchase a house in the town, primarily driven by Hemeve's role in overseeing their newly established auto shop adjacent to Smith's General Store. This strategic move allowed Hemeve to manage its operations more effectively. Meanwhile, Togora's brothers, Cypress and Dusk, continued to reside at the countryside home. Taking on substantial responsibilities, they became the driving force behind manufacturing the essential electrolytic solution, carefully bottling it in glass jars. Despite their youthful age, Cypress and Dusk displayed remarkable dedication in producing these potent cells.

Their efforts extended beyond manufacturing, as they also upgraded the existing water wheel at the riverhouse. This enhanced water wheel played a dual role – it powered an additional dynamo, specifically used to charge the battery cells before transporting them to the auto shop for retail.

Hemeve's electric vehicles stood out as a remarkable invention, contributing significantly to the growing automobile industry. Her reputation in the field of manufacturing became a primary part of life in Parsons Town.

The busy auto shop, with all its employees expertly trained by Hemeve, was running well. However, that year, Hemeve made the decision to spend the summer back at the countryside farm, allowing her to stay in close proximity to her workshop. During this time, she had been dedicated to refining her concept of a portable water wheel and devising a novel approach to charging the vehicles. This was driven by the fact that the dynamos at the riverhouse were already being extensively used by other applications.

Employing her adept woodworking talents, Hemeve sketched out the plans for a portable water wheel, encasing it within a protective enclosure and incorporating water inlet and outlet ports. She called her creation the "turbine," which would eventually be colloquially referred to as the "turbo." To evaluate its viability, Hemeve conducted preliminary tests by linking the water turbine to the hose that she used to irrigate her garden plants.

Through a close integration with a compact dynamo, the water turbine demonstrated its capability to produce significant electrical current. This allowed Hemeve's electric vehicle to recharge overnight while she attended to her vegetable irrigation routine. Hemeve cleverly modified the garden hose, crafting a cross-sectional opening. This original design permitted her vehicle, when connected to the hose, to harness the water turbine's energy, automatically charging as a convenient byproduct of her garden activities.

Hemeve found satisfaction in her revolutionary turbine-dynamo coupling; yet, two significant challenges remained in her pursuit of efficiency. The water pressure from her garden hose proved inadequate to drive the turbine at the optimal speed needed for generating the desired electrical output from the dynamo. Consequently, the vehicle received only partial charging by the next morning. Additionally, the charging process was using more water than necessary, impacting her ability to effectively irrigate her plants.

Hemeve dedicated months to contemplating potential solutions. Drawing inspiration from an irrigation article in the Almanac of Knowledge and adapting the concept to her situation, she formulated a solution: mounting a system of pipes in the river's path to redirect its flow. These pipes could then be carried away from the river's edge and positioned on the adjacent shoreline. The pipes varied in diameter, with the largest positioned at the river's source and progressively smaller pipes laid along its course. This arrangement naturally amplified the water pressure within the pipes.

The outcome of Hemeve's initial experiment proved to be impressive. The water jet that emerged from the other end of the pipe was notably stronger than the flow from her usual garden hose. The increased pressure from the modified setup was clear and promising.

Hemeve cleverly repurposed some tarp, normally used for drying grains, to make a pair of sturdy canvas hoses. One of these hoses was affixed to the terminal of the pipe from which the forceful water jet surged. This first hose was then linked to the inlet of her newly devised water turbine. The second canvas hose, stemming from the turbine's outlet, was looped back into the river's flow. Through this configuration, Hemeve amplified the water pressure requisite for the turbine's optimal performance and eliminated excessive water usage. The surplus water, instead of going to waste, was cleverly rerouted back into the river's current.

Hemeve carved wooden connectors for the extremities of the hoses and the corresponding ports on the turbine. These connectors served as templates, allowing Smith to craft identical cast iron replicas. Smith also crafted a replica of the wooden turbine, which has now become a sturdy and well-rounded piece.

Hemeve incorporated a water register at the pipe's termination to manage water flow and facilitate hose attachment when water wasn't running. Once all connections were established, Hemeve opened the register to enable water flow, propelling the turbine. Parked near the riverhouse, her auto cart could quickly connect or disconnect, ensuring her vehicle was fully charged each morning.

Chapter 5

Hydro Cart Technology: Revolutionizing Transportation

Upon perfecting her hydro charging station, Hemeve and Norde found themselves with their original cart and two additional carts requiring daily charging. Hemeve utilized one cart, while Cypress and Dusk used the other to transport glass jars filled with charged electrolytic solution.

Hemeve extended her invention further by creating additional fabric hoses using the tarp canvas, all equipped with cast iron quick connectors. She connected all three vehicles in series. Instead of directing the hose exiting the turbine of her vehicle into the river, she connected it to Norde's vehicle inlet port, and similarly in the case of Cypress and Dusk's vehicles. The outlet of the last vehicle was then directed back into the river, completing the circuit.

All three vehicles were fully charged by morning. Hemeve further refined the carts, relocating the inlet and outlet from the turbo box to the side of each vehicle. These were positioned side by side with a panel uniting both, featuring clear "In" and "Out" labels. She also integrated a set of tubes within the carts, extending from the side panel connectors to the location under each vehicle where the turbo-dynamo was situated.

Norde primarily resided in the townhouse while Hemeve dedicated more time to the farm due to her extensive hours in the workshop. Norde's bond with Smith grew stronger, spending considerable time together both at their respective workplaces, the general store, and the auto shop.

Smith, a seasoned traveler in pursuit of goods for his general store, frequently set out on business trips that spanned across various locales. One afternoon, while talking to Norde, Smith invited him to go on a trip to Black River City, a regional center in the nearby areas. This proposal presented an opportunity for Norde to venture beyond the familiar atmosphere of Parson's Town and gain insights into the broader economic landscape of the region.

With a sense of curiosity and a desire to expand his horizons, Norde eagerly accepted Smith's invitation. The journey promised to be a new experience, providing a firsthand look at the lively commerce, diverse markets, and interconnected trade routes that shaped the economic life of the region. As they embarked on their voyage, the landscape gradually shifted from the serene familiarity of Parson's Town to the vibrant center that was ahead.

During their trip, Norde had the chance to witness the network of suppliers, distributors, and merchants who contributed to the region's commercial drive. Smith's extensive knowledge of trade practices and his acquaintances along the way allowed Norde to glimpse the subtleties of sourcing goods and negotiating transactions.

The journey also offered moments of rapport and bond as Norde and Smith engaged in conversations that ranged from business strategies to the broader social fabric of the communities they encountered.

In the novel, the Almanac of Knowledge emerges as a significant promoter of change and modernization. This monthly publication becomes more than just a compendium of information; it serves as a wellspring of inspiration and empowerment for the characters, particularly Hemeve. Through its pages, Hemeve discovers a world of ideas, from efficient irrigation methods and farming principles to practical applications of electromagnetism. The almanac serves as a bridge between tradition and progress, guiding Hemeve's journey from talented carpentry to pioneering electric vehicles and hydro charging stations. Its articles inform and ignite the spark of curiosity and drive, prompting characters to improve their lives and their town through knowledge and resourceful thinking. The almanac brings together advancement, collaboration, and the pursuit of new horizons, ultimately shaping the destiny of Parson's Town and its residents.

During their trip to Black River City, Smith introduces Norde to a lively restaurant. As the evening grows, they indulge in drinks and a lavish dinner, the ambiance growing more intoxicating. However, the atmosphere takes a sudden turn as the lights dim, and a stage is revealed, adorned with a troupe of female dancers. The performance commences, a tantalizing display that gradually escalates with the dancers shedding their garments. Norde, conscious of his wife's disapproval, voices his intent to leave. Although swayed by Smith's insistence and their intoxicated state, they remain in the restaurant, drawn into the spectacle that takes place before them.

As the initial act concludes, an exceedingly attractive woman approaches the table where Smith and Norde are seated. She confidently positioned herself on Smith's lap, her tactile gestures tracing his physique. Norde's tension mounts significantly as he witnesses the woman engaging in an intimate kiss with Smith in the open setting. In swift sequence, another female dancer from the troupe joins them at the table, enveloping Norde from behind, her hands exploring his form. She inquires of Smith about Norde's identity, playfully referring to him as Smith's handsome companion.

Norde rises from his seat and heads towards the exit of the restaurant, now a nightclub, when he is intercepted by the woman who had approached him at the table earlier. She persistently urges him to remain for at least the duration of the next performance, as she is set to be the featured dancer on stage. Feeling increasingly uncomfortable, Norde agrees and returns to his seat, once again settling in to watch the alluring performance.

After the show concludes, both Norde and Smith make their way to the nearby hotel where they are staying for the night. They plan to spend the night there before heading back to Parson's Town the following morning.

Smith reassures Norde that everything is going well and advises him to relax and enjoy the night without worry, emphasizing that there's no one present who could reveal their secret to their wives back in Parson's Town.

As Norde stepped into the hotel room, the click of the door lock echoed a sense of seclusion, a safe place away from the dreamlike world they had just left behind. The dimmed lights of the room created a warm and inviting tone, creating a contrast to the vibrant and pulsating energy of the nightclub. Norde's mind was still confronting the wild turn of events that had taken place over the evening.

And then, from the depths of the room, emerged Angelica – the nightclub dancer, the very image of desire and the evening's extravagant events. Smith had orchestrated this surprise, his mischievous intentions concealed beneath his composed manner. The surprising appearance of Angelica in the hotel room sent a surge of confusion through Norde's veins, his thoughts racing to catch up with the facts.

The air seemed to thicken as Angelica moved gracefully toward him, her eyes sparkling with a blend of playfulness and enchantment. Her presence was mesmerizing. The forbidden thrill they had indulged in, the charm of secrecy drawing them deeper into the vortex of the unknown. Norde's heart pounded erratically, apprehension turning within him.

Smith's voice repeated in Norde's mind, urging him to embrace the moment, to let go of inhibitions and relish the emerging scenario. A surge of conflicting emotions gripped Norde – the responsibility as a husband and father, conflicting with the prospects of an escapade that challenged convention.

As Angelica drew nearer, her movements perfectly combining charm and confidence, Norde found himself caught between the thrill of the moment and the responsibilities of his commitments. Her presence seemed to fill the room. Smith's reassurances reverberated in Norde's ears, amplifying the hypnotic pull of the forbidden.

Norde's gaze locked onto Angelica's eyes, revealing the depth of his attraction.

As the night's events settled around them, Norde's mind was a storm of conflicting desires – the comfort of his familial bonds warring with the temptation of this unpredictable circumstance.

PART II

Chapter 6

CONFLICTING DESIRES, TEMPTATION, BURDENED REFLECTIONS

As Norde took a step towards the door, his resolve firm, he intended to end this odd encounter and step back into his life. However, Angelica's movements were swift and determined, revealing her persistence in pursuing her agenda. She stood before the door, an intimidating barrier between urge and control.

In the hushed hotel room, Angelica's voice held a seductive undertone, as she continued to weave her enchanting words, each syllable promising excitement and pleasure. Norde's conflict was clear, battling between constraint and the irresistible pull of this forbidden encounter.

Hesitation spread across Norde's features. Angelica's charm seemed to intensify in the intimate atmosphere, her words suggesting a path away from the constraints of his everyday life. As Angelica closed the distance, Norde felt her presence like a rush of emotions. The weight of responsibilities momentarily lifted, replaced by the overwhelming possibility of pleasure. Moments hung suspended, playing between consent and reproach.

With guilt and excitement, Norde gave in to Angelica's allure. Boundaries dissolved as he embraced this irresistible woman.

The night continued in whispers and sighs, secrecy deepening their intimacy. Hours slipped by like stolen moments, each touch manifesting their attraction. The room held their secrets, sharing desires that shielded them from the world.

As dawn's first light entered through the curtains, Norde awoke to an empty room, his heart heavy with guilt and regret. Traces of Angelica's presence lingered, as bittersweet evidence of the night's transgressions.

The room, once a place of ecstasy, now witnessed the duplicity of human nature – the collision of yearning and responsibility, desire and consequence. Norde stood at a crossroads, heart, and mind reflecting on a night that erased the lines between virtue and vice. The events of the previous night weighed deeply on his mind, leaving him with regret and uncertainty.

As he and Smith began their journey back to Parson in the afternoon, the atmosphere between them was tense, filled with silent thoughts and half-words. Despite the desire to address the situation, both men avoided the topic, allowing the memory of Angelica's surprising visit to remain hidden beneath the surface. The passing landscapes seemed to mirror Norde's struggle.

The hours on the road were marked by awkward silences and fleeting glances, each moment carrying the effects of what had transpired. Norde's gaze would occasionally drift to the world outside, attempting to distance himself from the charm that had led him astray. The fading light of the day evoked a melancholic aura, matching the profound emotions that had surfaced. As Parson came into view on the horizon, Norde carried the understanding that the road ahead would require courage and sincerity.

Returning to the familiar surroundings of Parson, Norde knew that his friendship with Smith had been tested. The silence between them spoke volumes, indicating the hidden truths that lingered. The journey ahead would be one of reflection and reconsideration. As Norde stepped back into the world he knew, he carried with him the determination to navigate the path ahead with honesty and clarity.

Upon their return to Parson, Jamela's mother and Hemeve found themselves engaged in a conversation outside the popular auto shop. With the anticipation of Smith and Norde's arrival from their trip to Black River City, the two women stood there, their voices blending with the ambient sounds of the town. The sun radiated a warm glow, creating a tranquil setting for their conversation as they exchanged stories and updates about their lives since the men's departure. Hemeve's eyes sparkled with the excitement of sharing her latest improvements, while Jamela's mother displayed curiosity and contentment, eager to hear the tales that were sure to captivate her.

As they finally arrived, Smith had a thoughtful surprise in hand, a gift he had obtained during their day's journey, intended for Jamela's mother, his beloved wife. The gesture filled the air with a sense of delight, as the gift became the centerpiece of attention upon their return. The excitement was noticeable, with Jamela's mother glowing with happiness, her gratitude evident in her eyes and warm smile. Amid this cheerful scene, Norde stood somewhat reserved, his manner hinting at a distraction that seemed to occupy his thoughts. In contrast to the lively chatter around him, he offered only brief responses, his gaze avoiding direct contact as if his mind wandered elsewhere.

Observing Norde's quiet demeanor, Hemeve, with her characteristic enthusiasm, proposed a drive back to their countryside home. She sensed that there was something on his mind that he wanted to share, and Norde consented to the trip. As they traveled, to alleviate the silence that started to build up, Hemeve began to tell Norde the idea she had had the day before, while he was away. With enthusiasm clear in her voice she revealed her plans to enhance the hydro charging station, the project that had ignited her creativity. Hemeve's excitement was evident as she described her vision — planning to build new wooden models, which would serve as templates for casting iron parts to support the charging infrastructure. This original idea seemed to spark a new drive within her, as she shared her aspirations with Norde during their ride back home.

Having returned to the tranquility of their countryside residence, Hemeve moved into her routine, preparing dinner and going about her tasks with her characteristic grace. As the evening developed, a sense of ease settled over Norde, releasing the tension he had carried from the trip. Hemeve's genuine and simple manner provided him relief. As the night drew near, the atmosphere between them softened, and their interactions became a reaffirmation of their profound connection. In the intimacy of their bedroom, surrounded by familiarity and warmth, Norde and Hemeve renewed their wedding vows — encapsulating their enduring love and commitment.

Chapter 7

ORIGINAL SOLUTIONS: REVEALING NATURE'S PRACTICALITY

Hemeve's visionary concept blossomed as she shared it with Norde within the peaceful setting of their countryside dwelling. Envisioning a more efficient future for their hydro charging station, she designed an integrated combination of key components. Her creative plan involved merging the shut-off valve, responsible for regulating the river water flow, with two of the cast iron quick connectors — one positioned at the exit point of the powerful water jet, and the other linked to the hose that returned the water to the river's embrace.

By crafting this combined iron cast mechanism, Hemeve aimed to streamline the operation of the charging station. This integration would enhance the system's performance and simplify its functionality. The shut-off valve, important for controlling water supply, would easily blend with the connectors, creating a fundamental and efficient mechanism. With her understanding of irrigation and practicality, Hemeve's idea held the promise of optimizing its hydro charging process.

The day before Norde's return, Hemeve found herself immersed in the serenity of her garden, enjoying freshly picked fruits. As she sliced one of the apples in two, a remarkable sight appeared before her eyes — the halves revealed an impressive resemblance to the cross-sectional view of a water pipe. An almost radiant partition emerged naturally within the heart of the fruit, reminiscent of a dividing wall.

This serendipitous observation, though apparently inconsequential, ignited a spark of inspiration within

Hemeve's imaginative mind. Drawing parallels between the organic configuration of the fruit's interior and the engineered design of water pipes, she recognized the potential for an original perspective. Such moments of serendipity often form the foundation of groundbreaking ideas. In this blended convergence of nature's design and human creativity, Hemeve's keen observation and creative imagination flourished, setting the stage for her inventive pursuit.

Within her contemplation, Hemeve's mind created patterns of possibility. The thought of a perpendicular pipe intersecting the main flow of water, creating an inverted "T" configuration, became the foundation of her inventive idea. She envisioned this secondary pipe as a passage, and as a variable element, with the potential to alter the course of the water's journey. The heart of her concept lay in a dividing wall, which emerged as an inspired continuation mechanism — a brilliant gate capable of controlling the flow of water.

With each detail that formed in her mind, Hemeve's excitement grew. The idea of a gate, ready within the perpendicular pipe, rang true. This gate, when lowered, could elegantly interrupt the passage of water, channeling it into an entirely new trajectory. As the pieces of her concept were put into place, it was as if she was making history in the world of water and transportation — a new way to harness the natural force of the river to generate electricity.

Amidst the abundant embrace of her garden, Hemeve's vision actualized. The collaboration between her observations of the fruit's inner shape and her understanding of waterworks evoked a sense of originality. In her mind, the once simple image of a halved fruit had blossomed into a clever solution — an elemental bridge between the organic world and her inventive mind.

Hemeve's imagination created a connection between separated elements. She also found inspiration in the threaded rods of the horse-drawn plow. The rods took on a new life, linking with her evolving idea. With a rod serving as a center of practicality, Hemeve envisioned a turning mechanism — a simple but effective means of controlling the gate within the perpendicular pipe.

Her mind painted a vivid scene: a wrench turning, threads engaging, and the gate gracefully responding to the guiding hand of the operator. The image of a threaded rod linked to the movable gate brought a sense of completion to the appliance she envisioned. This combination of nature and creativity felt like a flash of understanding.

In this way, Hemeve's mind connected the separated elements of pipes, rods, gates, and the powerful currents of the river. From the imaginary to the mundane, every piece fit together fluently in her vision.

Hemeve continued to refine her idea. She put two holes with nozzles on opposite sides of the perpendicular pipe's top part, right where the quick connectors were attached. Each hole was connected to one side of the pipe's inner wall. She also created a strong cap to cover the top of the perpendicular pipe. This cap would keep everything secure and in place. Her mind was more than sharp, putting all the pieces together to make her idea work. It was a simple and clever design that felt like it would facilitate the charging process.

Hemeve and Smith delved into the practicality of casting the iron parts. In just a few days, Hemeve had wooden models ready, which Smith used to create the final cast iron pieces. They incorporated flanges into the design, giving them dimensions easily connectable to the existing pipes commonly used in city works. The collaboration between Hemeve's inventive thinking and Smith's casting talents proved to be a successful partnership.

With Smith's expertise, they transformed the extending end of the threaded rod into an easily rotating bolt, designed with double threading concentrically to the rod. Hemeve also made a wooden wrench along with two caps for the nozzles, effectively sealing the open ports. This functional mechanism demonstrated their attention to detail and their commitment to manifesting their original idea.

In a straightforward manner, Smith utilized a wooden box filled with sand to cast the new iron parts based on the models Hemeve had designed in her workshop. After a short waiting period, the parts were completed and transported to Hemeve's rural residence. With the dedicated assistance of the two employees, the valve installation process started. To ensure a suitable environment for the installation, they thoughtfully covered the pipe's entrance with a tarp, creating a dry and functional workspace for the important task. Positioned at the end of the pipe where the fabric hose used to be connected, the new valve was carefully put into place.

Hemeve's creative thinking and Smith's practiced craftsmanship blended effectively during this phase. Hemeve's initial idea, built into actual models, was brought to life by Smith's casting expertise. The results were the newly cast iron parts ready to replace the former components. Guided by Hemeve's insightful vision and Smith's practical execution, their joint effort ensured that the valve was securely integrated into the system.

Chapter 8

Integrating Precision: Hydro Charging Station

Hemeve's approach continued as she carefully integrated the gate mechanism into the valve's body. Ensuring a secure attachment, she adeptly affixed the rod to the mechanism. The threaded head cap found its place atop the valve, firmly locked in position by the revolving bolt. She affixed the two threaded caps onto the valve's nozzles, completing the assembly with precision. To finalize the installation, Hemeve utilized flanges and bolts to connect the valve to the pipe, guaranteeing a sturdy and reliable connection.

Hemeve's attention to detail and proficiency in implementing her design was evident in each step of the valve's creation and installation. With precision, she conducted the integration of various parts, securing them in place for optimal functionality.

Positioning her hydro cart adjacent to the newly installed valve, Hemeve retrieved the folded fabric hoses stored in the cart's trunk. With swift precision, she proceeded to connect the hoses, guided by the clearly labeled signs displayed on the connectors' faceplate. These connectors were mounted to the vehicle's side, emulating the corresponding connections on her newly installed valve. The alignment was true, a perfect fit that complemented each other precisely. Following this process, they revealed the pipe's mouth at the river's top, removing the tarp that shielded it. As they did so, the mounting pressure within the pipe and the valve began to build.

Hemeve's ability to merge practical engineering with thoughtful design manifested in this important moment, promising a functional and efficient hydro station for her electric vehicles.

Taking the cast iron wrench that she had carefully designed, Hemeve prepared to execute the next important step. With a strong sense of purpose, her fingers found their grip on the custom-made tool. The wrench was part of the manifestation of her invention, representing the means to activate the valve.

As Hemeve turned the wrench with measured determination, a sense of anticipation filled the air. Its motion reflected her deliberate intent, setting in motion a sequence of events that would bring her creation to life. As she applied pressure and continued to turn, the mechanism within the valve responded. With each incremental quarter-turn of the wrench, the machinery hummed to life, allowing the water to flow into her vehicle.

The turning of the wrench was an act that celebrated the transition from concept to actuality, initiating the gradual transfer of water from the flowing river to the eagerly awaiting hoses of the hydro cart. This important act marked the beginning of a system that promised to enhance the efficiency of her charging station.

Hemeve called her resourceful creation a hydrant, aligning its name with the essence of her hydro cart. The name had a purpose; it encapsulated the core of her concept, drawing a direct connection to water as the fundamental source of kinetic energy driving the process of generating electricity. This choice of name illuminated the foundation of her invention, emphasizing the central role of water in her groundbreaking system. With the introduction of the hydrant valve, Hemeve solidified her idea in a concise and meaningful term.

The riverside station where her hydro cart was charged became commonly known as the hydrant station. This name reflected the essence of the technology and its connection to water-driven energy. Through her creative naming, Hemeve naturally integrated her invention into everyday language, promoting a clear understanding of the purpose and functionality of her system.

Drawing upon the collaboration of Smith, Hemeve's expertise extended to providing quick-connect options for the other vehicles within her household. With Smith's assistance, she reproduced her concept, casting two additional valves to facilitate the efficient connection of her other vehicles to the hydrant station. This expansion demonstrated the adaptability and scalability of her invention, catering to the growing demand and ensuring that her creative solution could be easily integrated into various applications.

Upon Smith's insightful suggestion, Hemeve recognized the value of documenting her creation for broader sharing. Taking heed of this advice, she systematically detailed every aspect of the hydrant's design and operation, ensuring a comprehensive understanding of her invention. With her documentation in hand, Hemeve promptly sent her insights to the offices of the Almanac of Knowledge. Within a remarkably short span, her diligent efforts yielded fruit as the publication responded with an official plan of the hydrant's inner workings, complete with instructions for its assembly.

The inclusion of her invention in the pages of the Almanac marked a significant milestone for Hemeve. It offered an actual form of recognition for her contribution and marked the memorable impact her creation could have on a broader scale. By sharing her invention through the widely read Almanac of Knowledge, Hemeve ensured that her concept would go beyond her immediate circumstances and potentially inspire others to explore the territories of water-driven transportation. Through her initiative, Hemeve solidified her place in a legacy of originality, securing a lasting testament to her dedication to progress and improvement.

Chapter 9

PROCUREMENT CHALLENGES: INFLUENCE, FAIRNESS, TRANSPARENCY

Coinciding with these significant events, positive changes continued to sweep through Norde's life. His dedication and commitment to public service were rewarded with a notable promotion, propelling him to the esteemed position of Chief of Procurements and Purchases for Parson's Town City Hall. This new responsibility placed him at the forefront of ensuring the steady functioning of essential city operations.

Simultaneously, Parson's Town embarked on an important project to enhance its infrastructure. With an eye towards enhancing the efficiency of water distribution throughout the city, they initiated a substantial procurement process. The city announced an extensive competition, inviting businesses from the region to bid for the opportunity to provide a significant quantity of iron pipes — an important component in expanding the city's water distribution network.

As Norde took on his elevated role, the convergence of his professional trajectory and the city's infrastructure development became apparent. His newfound position granted him an exclusive vantage point to contribute to the progression of Parson's Town. With his expertise in procurement, Norde was well-positioned to navigate the details of the competitive process and make impactful decisions for the city's benefit. The synchronicity of these events demonstrated the relationship of personal and communal progress, underlining Norde's important role in shaping the future of Parson's Town.

In a moment of private conversation, Smith approaches Norde with a combination of eagerness and concern. He expresses his ardent desire to secure the important procurement for the cast iron pipes from Parson's Town city hall. Aware of Norde's influential role in the city's procurement process, Smith seeks his assistance to navigate the competitive landscape and support his chances of success. He confides in Norde about the impending threat posed by a newly established foundry in town, one that specializes in public works. Smith's apprehension comes from the realization that this emerging competitor could potentially outshine his own bid for the procurement.

Smith's anxiety is obvious as he outlines the stakes of the situation. He shares with Norde the exceptional situation at play, emphasizing the pressure he is facing from his associates based in Black River City. Their ardent interest in securing the procurement reveals a larger strategy: by clinching the sale of the iron pipes to Parson's Town, they aim to fortify their foundry business, specializing in city infrastructure projects.

Smith's aspirations face an abrupt setback as Norde, openly and with a sense of duty, delivers news that dashes his expectations. Norde, fully aware of the ethical implications of his new role at the city hall, informs Smith that the procurement process must remain just and fair. In an open exchange, Norde explains that his recent promotion brings with it the responsibility to ensure fairness and transparency in the selection of bids for the city contract.

In this important moment, Norde emphasizes his commitment to upholding the integrity of the procurement process. He acknowledges that his position comes with a heightened level of scrutiny, requiring him to avoid even the appearance of favoritism or conflict of interest. This recognition carries a profound responsibility, revealing Norde's dedication to the principles of public service and ethical conduct.

Smith's intentions collide with the actuality of the situation, as he contends with the realization that Norde's hands are tied when it comes to influencing the selection process.

With a determined focus on maintaining a fair concurrence, Norde diligently arranges meetings with the eight qualified bidders competing for the procurement contract, which includes Smith's bid. In a series of structured sessions, Norde offers each of the contenders an opportunity to present their businesses and substantiate the merits of their bids.

During these interactions, the competing parties step into the spotlight, introducing themselves and their companies. With a combination of confidence, ambition, and professionalism, they outline their capabilities and articulate how their respective offerings align with the city's requirements. The meetings serve as a platform for the bidders to elaborate on their strengths, share case studies, and provide actual evidence supporting their proposals.

As the discussions proceed, Norde maintains an even-handed approach, carefully considering each presentation without bias or prejudice. His role as an impartial facilitator becomes evident as he listens attentively, asking insightful questions that prompt bidders to delve deeper into the specifics of their bids. By promoting an environment of fairness and open dialogue, Norde ensures that all contenders have a fair chance to showcase their potential contributions to the city's needs.

The process allows the bidders to make their case and showcases Norde's dedication to conducting a thorough evaluation. Through these meetings, Norde demonstrates his commitment to upholding a level playing field for all parties involved, setting the stage for a fair decision-making process that will ultimately determine the recipient of the procurement contract.

As the completion of the procurement evaluation process approaches, the final meeting is scheduled with A. Glen, the representative of Brothers Alliance, a traditional business based in Black River aiming to make its mark in the business of city contracts. The meeting is set to take place at ten o'clock in the morning, setting the first activity of Norde's day in the town hall.

Anticipation fills the air as the appointed time draws near. The town hall ruffles with the sound of administrative activity, punctuated by the knowledge that this meeting holds the potential to shape the future course of city projects. Norde, now a key figure in Parson's Town city hall, prepares to engage in the essential conversation that will finalize the decision on the procurement contract.

In this important moment, Norde's role as a facilitator of fair evaluation and honest decision-making takes center stage. The meeting with A. Glen from Brothers Alliance encapsulates the essence of the entire procurement process, reflecting Norde's dedication to ensuring that all qualified bidders have an equal opportunity to present their case and demonstrate their potential to contribute to the city's growth and progress.

PART III

Chapter 10

INTERSECTIONS: WOMEN, SECRETS, AND ENCOUNTERS

Norde is busy in his office when his secretary enters, informing him that Ms. Glen is present and awaiting his attention. The mention of Ms. Glen as the representative from Brothers Alliance catches Norde by surprise.

The fact that a woman stands as a key figure representing a business in a competitive procurement process speaks volumes about the changing tides.

With Hemeve's remarkable creativity and visionary spirit in mind, Norde recognizes that the eighteen hundreds ushered in a period where gender barriers were gradually dismantling.

Leaving his office desk, Norde walks through the corridors of the town hall, making his way to the waiting area where his secretary is seated. He intends to greet Ms. Glen, the representative from Brothers Alliance, who is waiting there for their meeting. In contrast, what happens before him takes him by surprise.

As he approaches the waiting area, Norde's eyes widen as he recognizes the person standing beside his secretary. It's Angelica, the woman he encountered during his ill-advised escapade at the nightclub in Black River. The memories of that night come rushing back, mingling with the truth of the situation. Norde's heart races as he struggles to process this abrupt convergence of events.

Caught in a moment of shock, Norde finds himself at a crossroads. On one side stands his commitment to professional conduct and the evaluation of bids, while on the other looms the haunt of his personal misstep. His thoughts race, contending with the interplay of his professional and personal lives that now seem to have collided in the most unpredicted of circumstances.

With Angelica waiting to discuss the bid from Brothers Alliance and anticipating their meeting, Norde must navigate this delicate situation with discretion and composure. The meeting that was meant to be a routine part of his day has changed into a challenging interplay of emotions.

Alone in his office with Angelica, the air grows heavy with the confession she is about to make.

As she begins to speak, Angelica's words carry a chilling undertone. She reveals that their encounter that fateful night at the hotel had less privacy than Norde believed. In a shockingly calculated move, Angelica discloses that she had an accomplice hidden in the hotel room, capturing their intimate moments on camera. The implications of her disclosure strike Norde like a lightning bolt.

With a malicious smile, Angelica presents Norde with the compromising photographs that could shatter his world. The images lay bare the private moments he shared with her, leaving him exposed to potential ruin. The threat is clear: if Smith's bid doesn't secure the procurement, these photographs will find their way to Hemeve, his wife, forever altering the course of their lives.

Walking a tightrope, Norde is faced with an excruciating decision. The balance between his professional integrity, his personal life, and the threat of public humiliation hangs in the air like a heavy cloud. The photographs in Angelica's hands wield the power to unravel everything he holds dear, leaving him confronting the most daunting choice he has ever faced. In this tense encounter, the paths he must navigate become hauntingly true.

As the situation settles over Norde, he wrestles with the demands Angelica has placed upon him. The stakes have been raised. Her insistence on meeting for dinner that very night adds a layer of urgency to the growing drama. Norde, deeply troubled by the ramifications of his past actions, finds himself cornered between his marital vows and the blackmail that now hangs over him.

In a tense exchange, Norde attempts to reason with Angelica, explaining the gravity of his marital commitment and the mistake that their encounter made. However, Angelica's anger and frustration grow apparent, thundering through the walls of Norde's office. The emotional unrest within the confined space only heightens Norde's anxiety, conscious of his secretary's close proximity and the potential for his private affair to become public knowledge.

Faced with a rapidly escalating situation and under a cloud of uncertainty, Norde takes a decisive step. He requests a city hall courier to travel to his countryside home and inform Hemeve of a fabricated story. He creates a tale of needing to help Smith after work with some reports for the general store, using it as a cover to explain his absence. Norde plans this will provide him the opportunity to meet Angelica that night without raising Hemeve's suspicions.

The night arrives, and Norde finds himself standing before his own townhouse. As he opens the door to greet Angelica, the price of his choices, secrets, and the potential fallout deceitfully rests profoundly on his shoulders. In this important moment, Norde's life is ready on the edge of a precipice.

As Norde stands on the porch of his townhouse, he is greeted by a transformed Angelica. Her beauty, always apparent, seems to have been elevated to new heights on this particular night. With attention to detail, she has adorned her appearance to leave a lasting impression. Her slender figure and striking features combine to create an aura that commands attention in any setting.

As the door opens, revealing Angelica's captivating presence, anticipation surges through Norde. The memories of their previous encounter in Black River mingle with the strain of the present situation. Her radiant smile, though laced with a hint of malice, holds an attraction that he finds difficult to resist.

The atmosphere within the townhouse is charged with excitement, nervousness, and an underlying tension. Norde's struggle intensifies as he contends with the inevitable implications of the situation. He is aware of the choices he has made and the network of secrets that now threatens to unravel. In this important moment, as he faces Angelica once again, the boundaries between impulse, restraint, and the repercussions of his decisions become increasingly blurred.

Chapter 11

DESIRES, ETHICAL DILEMMAS, AND TEMPTATIONS

In the confined space of the townhouse, the intimate atmosphere ignites an irresistible pull between Norde and Angelica. As the door closes behind them, they are enveloped by an aura of secrecy that seems to erase all other considerations. In a matter of seconds, the boundaries are swept aside, and their bodies draw close with urgency and anticipation.

Their embrace, filled with excitement, happens near the entrance. At this moment, the world outside seems to fade into insignificance as their desires take center stage. The burden of consequences momentarily loses its grip.

In the distress of their passion, Norde and Angelica share an intimacy that is deep and profound. Their actions are driven by a potent secrecy, and an intense urge to momentarily give in to their impulses. The townhouse becomes a hideaway for their most unrestrained feelings and desires.

In the intimate afterglow of their encounter, Angelica's words carry a tone that goes beyond the physical closeness they've just shared. Her confession catches Norde off guard, stirring a mixture of emotions within him. As they lay there, their insecurities exposed, Angelica's straightforwardness forces him to confront the feelings that he had been attempting to suppress.

Her admission of liking him rings true in the air, and for a moment, the space around them seems suspended, their shared emotions forging a silent connection. Norde argues with his own emotions, his struggle evident in his crumpled brow and searching gaze. He wrestles with the implications of her invitation to Black River, torn between his commitment to his wife and the wanting of this newfound connection.

Angelica's leverage becomes apparent. It's an inescapable fact, even as he yearns to. The delicate balance of power tips in her favor, and Norde's hesitation is unmistakable. Despite his conflict, he senses the inevitability of the situation she has presented to him, a situation that could potentially shatter the life he has carefully built.

As their conversation progresses in the hushed intimacy of the night, Norde's resolve is put to the test. He's caught in an attachment of desire and manipulation that could alter the trajectory of his life.

The morning light filters through the windows, casting a soft glow on the aftermath of the night. As Angelica prepares to leave, Norde's thoughts are a tumultuous cloud of guilt and regret. He watches her go, stirring emotions within him.

In the quiet of the townhouse, Norde is left alone with his thoughts. The events of the previous night weigh intensely on his conscience as he confronts the ethical dilemma that now engulfs him. The memories form a knot of trepidation in the pit of his stomach.

Norde struggles with the truth of his infidelity and the impending compromise of his integrity at work. The two transgressions, interrelated although distinct, become a heavy burden he must bear. He paces the room, his footsteps reflecting the confusion within his mind.

As the morning advances, Norde is faced with a judgment. The moral principle that once guided him is now clouded by the entanglements of his desires and the truth of the situation he finds himself in.

With a heavy sigh, Norde knows that the repercussions of his decisions are inevitable. The path he's chosen, both in matters of the heart and in matters of ethics, has set him on a course that will test his values and integrity. The morning sun illuminates the room, casting shadows that reflect what now lingers in his conscience.

Norde stands there, with shock painted across his face as he listens to Smith's words. The air around them seems to grow heavy with the burden of the disclosure. The half-joking remark feels like a cold gust of truth, confirming the manipulation that had been arranged behind his back.

As Smith continues to explain the details of the scheme, Norde's mind races to make sense of it all. The idea of being part of a calculated plan, a chess piece moved according to someone else's agenda, leaves him feeling a blend of anger and helplessness. The very foundation of trust he had held with Smith has been shaken to its core.

The awareness of the bank account in his name feels like a trap closing in on him. Norde envisions the account as bait for what he is now forced to do. The promise of a substantial deposit in exchange for a contract bid feels like a Faustian bargain, a deal that could grant him financial gains at the cost of his principles.

A surge of conflicting emotions curls within Norde. The choice before him seems to be one of personal advantage versus professional ethics. The sense of being caught in a net of deceit consumes him, and he battles with the question of whether he can release himself from the plot that has been spun around him.

In the center of the busy store, Norde stands face to face with the choice that will define his character. As he absorbs the severity of Smith's disclosures, he knows that the path ahead is filled with challenges and moral dilemmas. The brotherhood's offer, once evidently tempting, now looms as a test of his integrity and the values he holds dear.

Norde's heart sinks even further as Smith acknowledges the trap that has been set for him. The ultimatum extends beyond mere financial gain and delves into the field of emotional manipulation. The threat to tarnish Hemeve's trust and their marriage with the compromising pictures strikes a chord deep within Norde.

The aftermath of the choice he faces becomes almost suffocating. On one side, there's the temptation of monetary gain, a tempting prospect that could offer financial security and a more comfortable lifestyle. On the other side is his love for Hemeve, their bond that has weathered a plethora of storms and victories. The mere thought of betraying her trust and the vows of their relationship is a heavy burden to bear.

Norde's mind races through the options, his moral compass guiding him through a labyrinth of decisions. The temptation to yield, to give in to the brotherhood's demands, is a fierce battle within him. Yet, the thought of Hemeve's pain, of her disappointment and hurt, pierces through the fog of uncertainty.

Chapter 12

Ordinary Shadows:

Norde's Story

Norde's heart is heavy as he makes the fateful decision to yield to the brotherhood's demands. The weight of his choice is like an anchor, pulling him deeper into a bond of deceit and betrayal. He knows that what he's doing is wrong, that he's compromising his values and his marriage, and that fear has clouded his judgment.

As he meets Angelica in Black River, guilt consumes him. The newfound secrecy of their meetings is a contrast to the transparency and trust he shared with Hemeve. The house he purchases under Angelica's name becomes a symbol of his duplicity, a physical manifestation of the distance he's creating between himself and his true life.

Each encounter with Angelica is bittersweet, tainted by the knowledge of his betrayal. The allure of the forbidden and the excitement of their meetings are dominated by the guilt that corrodes within him. Norde's actions haunt him.

As time goes on, the pressure of his secrets becomes unbearable. The façade he's constructed begins to crumble under the strain. The once-solid foundation of his life is now cracked, and the trust he had with Hemeve is eroding. The path he's chosen has led him to a crossroads, where he must confront his mistakes and decide if he has the strength to set things straight.

Norde's downward spiral continues as he yields to the pressure of the brotherhood. Granting Smith two more city contracts only deepens his involvement in the unethical dealings, further compromising his integrity. The once-respected man finds himself mired in a cycle of deceit and manipulation that compromises his reputation in Parson.

The city's perception of Norde shifts as rumors and whispers spread about his questionable decisions and associations. His reputation, once solid and respected, becomes tarnished and stained. Those who once looked up to him now regard him with skepticism and disappointment, and Norde can feel the effects of their judgment bearing down on him.

As the next city election arrives, Norde faces the results of the election that reveal the trust and confidence he once enjoyed from the community have deteriorated. He is replaced as the chief procurement officer, a position he had held with honor. It's a sobering moment for Norde, as he comes to terms with the fallout of his decisions.

The loss of his position serves as a wake-up call. Norde is left to reflect on the path he's taken, and the toll it's taken on his personal and professional life. He must find a way to regain his sense of self and his place within the community he once served.

Among the changing landscape of Parson's Town, Smith's store continues to flourish, fueled by the recent contracts secured through Norde's involvement. The trio – Smith, Hemeve, and Norde – engage in a conversation at the auto shop, a familiar space where they've shared innumerable discussions over the years. With Norde's recent loss of his city hall position, an idea emerges, one that might offer him a fresh start.

Recognizing Norde's experience and expertise in procurement, Smith proposes that Norde takes the reins for the purchasing operations at the general store. After deliberation and discussions, a decision is reached, and an agreement is sealed. In the presence of Hemeve, the pact is made – Norde will transition into this new role, a remarkable step in the journey of his character.

With his new role as the head of purchasing for Smith's busy general store, Norde finds himself with a legitimate reason to travel frequently to Black River. Unknowing to Hemeve, he seizes this opportunity to discreetly spend the money he had earned through the clandestine deals organized by the brotherhood. This secret fund had initially been used to buy a house in Black River under Angelica's name.

As Norde navigates his dual life, his visits to Black River become more frequent. The house he purchased becomes a hideout for his encounters with Angelica, a space where he can momentarily escape the complications of his responsibilities in Parson's Town. The money he receives from the brotherhood's contracts provides the means for him to finance these encounters and maintain his clandestine relationship.

Throughout this smoke screen of secrecy, Norde struggles. Despite his outward appearance of success and his new role in the general store, he is haunted by the guilt of his past actions, particularly as he continues to keep Hemeve in the dark about the true source of the funds that enabled him to enjoy a lavish lifestyle.

Word of Hemeve's groundbreaking invention, the hydrant, quickly spreads far and wide. The news of her success spread throughout Parson's Town and beyond, as her creative device captured the imagination of many. At the age of forty-eight, Hemeve's name became synonymous with breakthrough and invention, and her achievements led to a notable turning point in her life.

The Almanac of Knowledge, a publication renowned for celebrating pioneering advancements, selects Hemeve as the recipient of its prestigious Inventor of the Year award. This recognition is a tribute to the impact her invention has had on the collective. The honor is magnified by the fact that Hemeve is the first woman to ever grace the pages of the almanac with a personal profile, solidifying her place in history.

As the news spreads, Hemeve's reputation soars to new heights. People from all walks of life are captivated by her story – a tale of determination, originality, and resilience. She becomes an inspiration for young minds, encouraging them to pursue their passions. Hemeve's achievement benefits her personally and contributes to the ongoing progress and modernization of Parson's Town and the broader world.

Among the acclaim, Hemeve's legacy extends beyond her role as an inventor. She evolves into a symbol of empowerment for women and a beacon of hope for anyone with a vision to make a meaningful impact. Her remarkable journey from a housewife on a small farm to a renowned inventor shows that, with creativity and determination, one can shape the future and leave an enduring mark on history.

Chapter 13

A Hydro Cart Revolution

The mayor of Parson's Town is quick to recognize the significance of Hemeve's achievement and the impact of her hydrant invention. In a gesture that reflects the town's appreciation for her groundbreaking work, the mayor initiates a project to install eight hydrant valves in the town's park, situated alongside the river that has been a source of inspiration for Hemeve's inventions. This decision is a tribute to her accomplishments and a practical step toward promoting her creation.

These newly installed hydrants are a celebration of Hemeve's pioneering spirit and represent an actual contribution to the town and its residents. Positioned strategically in the park, the hydrants become a focal point where hydro cart owners can easily access the river's water source, integrating her invention into the daily lives of the townspeople. This initiative promotes a sense of community and collaboration among hydro cart owners, as they come together to celebrate Hemeve's talent and enjoy the convenience of her invention.

The installation of the hydrants also highlights the town's commitment to progress and modernization, embracing the benefits of technological advancements. Hemeve's impact on Parson's Town is evident in the physical presence of the hydrants and in the way her invention has transformed transportation. Her legacy lives on as hydro cart owners and the townspeople alike benefit from her pioneering work, and her story continues to inspire future generations to explore original solutions to pressing challenges.

Black River City derives its name from its strategic location adjacent to the shores of the Black River. This progressing urban center is divided into two distinct sections, situated on both the left and right banks of the river, which are interconnected by two sturdy bridges. The river itself holds immense significance for the city, serving as a vital lifeline that pulsates with activity and plays a central role in its active existence.

The river's vital role in Black River City is evident. It serves as the primary channel that supports the city's growth and prosperity, similar to a busy pathway that promotes the various aspects of urban life. The river's expansive presence influences the city's geography and shapes its economic, cultural, and social fabric. Industries, trade routes, and recreational activities are all elaborately meshed around the river's flowing currents.

Notably, the same river that courses through Parson's Town and meanders past Hemeve's countryside residence contributes its waters to the Black River. This connection emphasizes the relationship of these regions and highlights the importance of water bodies as unifying elements, binding different locales in a network of natural resources and shared environments. Just as rivers have historically been sources of life and nourishment, the Black River stands as a symbol of drive and growth for the city that draws its name from its majestic presence.

The Black River, situated alongside Black River City, functions as a vital transportation pathway for crucial commodities, chiefly iron ore and other essential materials.

These resources are efficiently transported through the river's waterways, reaching the heart of the urban center. Here, a large array of general stores, shops, and specialized establishments, including blacksmiths, strategically thrive, benefiting from the river's accessible trade route.

The river's role as a transportation channel is important in facilitating trade and commerce within the city. Its navigable waters provide a cost-effective means of moving bulky materials like iron minerals, thereby ensuring a consistent supply of essential resources to the city's core. This robust transportation network serves as an economic backbone, nurturing the growth of local industries and contributing to the city's overall prosperity.

Positioned along the river's edge, general stores and specialized shops are sophisticatedly connected to the flow of goods. The river's proximity enables the efficient distribution of products to these establishments, enabling them to provide for the diverse needs of both residents and businesses. Furthermore, the availability of iron and other transported materials supports the city's various manufacturing sectors, propelling their expansion and success.

Ultimately, the Black River emerges as a lifeline supporting the economic strength of Black River City. Its significance is in its role as both a channel for goods and a resource for urban development. The relationship of nature, transportation, and business demonstrates the prospering collaboration that defines this lively metropolis.

Word spreads to Parson's Town about the Mayor of Black River City's progressive collaboration with a local transportation company. Together, they have harnessed the power of hydro carts equipped with the revolutionary hydrant technology, initially conceptualized by Hemeve and featured in the Almanac of Knowledge. This forward-thinking initiative involves the establishment of a fleet comprising twelve hydro carts, specially designed for the efficient delivery of essential goods such as bottled milk, bread, ice, and fresh produce. These hydro carts navigate the busy downtown core, capitalizing on the efficiency and nature preservation offered by the hydrant technology.

Building upon Hemeve's pioneering work, the city has taken this concept further by incorporating thirty-two hydrant units within a park situated alongside the majestic river that winds through the heart of the city. This strategic placement of hydrant units reinforces the accessibility and convenience of the technology for both residents and visitors. With the city hall in close proximity, this park serves as a symbolic center of progress, showcasing the application of creativity into everyday urban life.

The evolution of the hydro cart concept, now paired with all-in-one units featuring Hemeve's hydroelectric turbine and a built-in dynamo, has sparked a growing market. The Almanac of Knowledge, alongside its team of expert engineers, has contributed to refining and perfecting the technology. This has given rise to an array of options, from maker kits for enthusiasts to pre-assembled units tailored for various applications, be it leisurely rides or the efficient transportation of goods. As manufacturers embrace these advancements, the landscape of urban transportation and commerce undergoes a transformative shift, setting the stage for a new period of public development.

As the years rolled on, the widespread adoption of hydro carts led to remarkable changes in urban infrastructure. Black River City, along with several other municipalities, embarked on an ambitious undertaking: the installation of extensive underground mains, running beneath the streets and avenues. These mains carried water from adjacent rivers, paralleling the existing potable water lines. This novel approach allowed the rivers to serve an important purpose, contributing to the city's hydro transportation water supply.

The integration of hydro cart technology brought about a notable surge in public transportation. Larger passenger hydro carts emerged, navigating the vibrant city centers with ease. These hydro carts became a preferred means of moving people quickly and efficiently through the vibrant urban cores. The transformation of rivers into hidden conduits for transportation marked a significant shift in city planning and development during the mid-eighteen hundreds.

The practice of river canalization, once a pioneering experiment in Black River City, quickly gained traction across various urban landscapes. Cities far and wide recognized the potential of utilizing waterways for more than just navigation. The brilliance of integrating transportation and water systems eased the movement of people and goods and showcased the remarkable adaptability of technology to shape the evolving urban environment.

PART IV

Chapter 14

Urban Mobility: Bonds, Trust, and Betrayal

The dedicated water mains, exclusively purposed from rivers, continued their expansion into the heart of urban areas. In this transformative landscape, water parks began to sprout up, each featuring well-placed hydrant stations tailored for the convenient boarding and exit of hydro trams. These trams offered an enjoyable mode of transportation, and their popularity was evident as they sold tickets for rides from strategically positioned stops within the busy urban centers.

The production of hydro vehicles, now often referred to as "cars," surged into a dynamic phase of growth. In a remarkably short span of time, notable advancements touched every component of these vehicles. The once rudimentary hydro carts evolved into sophisticated machines, featuring luxurious enclosed cockpits that provided comfort and protection. Advancements encompassed various aspects, including braking systems, gear-shifting mechanisms, and headlights to facilitate safe night driving. This rapid evolution catered to an expanding clientele, reflecting the growing demand for more refined and convenient transportation solutions.

As the landscape continued to evolve, the integration of hydro trams and the refinement of hydro vehicles created a profound shift in urban mobility. The improvement from simple river utilization to a full-fledged urban transportation system demonstrated the adaptability of technology in shaping the way people moved and lived in the rapidly changing cities of the period.

Norde's visits to Black River escalated in frequency, drawn deeper into a bond of compulsion by Angelica's insistent demands. With each encounter, he found himself increasingly entangled in her charm, giving in to her desires despite the moral upheaval within him. Angelica, influenced by Norde's generous gains from the deals he orchestrated during his permanence as the procurement officer for Parson's Town, experienced a transformation herself. She embraced a new style and personal appearance, an outward reflection of the lavish benefits derived from Norde's biased dealings that had favored his associate, Smith, the owner of the local general store.

Norde's journey into infidelity and ethical compromise weighed on him. The captivating promise of pleasure and indulgence provided by Angelica had clouded his judgment, leading him down a path of deceit and moral ambiguity. As he journeyed between Parson's Town and Black River, torn between his loyalty to his wife and family and the tempting desires that Angelica embodied.

Norde's overnight escapades evolved into extended stays, stretching for two or even three consecutive nights, and gradually, his presence in Parsons Town faded to the weekends alone. With each passing day spent away from his family, his connection with Hemeve began to fray, the warmth between them replaced by an unsettling chill. Norde's inability to share the truth of his activities weighed seriously on their interactions. The once open and honest relationship between husband and wife now carried the burden of secrets, creating an emotional chasm between them.

Hemeve, cleverly perceptive of the change in Norde's manner, sensed the growing distance between them. She could notice the shifting dispositions and the subtle signs that something was wrong. Worried by Norde's increasing reluctance to confide in her, Hemeve's concerns multiplied as she continued with the uncertainty clouding his behavior. She yearned for the days of sincerity and trust that had defined their relationship, yet the obscure shroud Norde had enveloped their interactions left her feeling isolated and in the dark.

As Norde's absence prolonged and his secrets increased, the foundation of their marriage weakened.

Norde's involvement with the Brothers Alliance deepened, as the members of the organization extended their influence into various aspects of his life. Recognizing his commitment, they welcomed him as an affiliate member into their fraternal fold. This affiliation carried weight, granting Norde a sense of belonging that connected with the charm of their promises. As his ties with the alliance grew, his connection to Parson's Town seemed to loosen, and he found himself drawn into a new period of his life.

In response to the widening horizon presented by the Brothers Alliance, Norde accepted an enticing high-paying job in Black River, shifting his priorities. The position demanded extensive travel, often requiring him to spend one or two weeks away from home. As he embarked on this new professional journey, his absence from Parson's Town became more prolonged, further disintegrating the threads that had once tightly bound him to his family and community.

The charm of this organization and the opportunities it presented drew him further away from his roots. His new career path, while financially rewarding, came at the cost of his presence in Parson's Town and his connection with Hemeve.

Returning unexpectedly to his home in Black River due to a canceled business trip, Norde stumbled upon a scene that shattered his sense of trust and security. To his disbelief, he discovered Smith and Angelica together in the very place he had thought was a retreat from his troubles. This shocking discovery exposed a web of deceit that had trapped him for much longer than he had imagined.

As Angelica revealed the truth before him, Norde's world crumbled. She confessed that her connection with Smith predated her involvement with him. The very foundation of their connection was tainted by Angelica's hidden history with Smith. Her admission laid bare her motivations and the manipulation that had taken place behind the scenes.

The disclosure left Norde confronted with a tumult of emotions - betrayal, anger, and humiliation. The realization that he had been a pawn in a larger game of deceit hit him hard, and he confronted the painful truth that his trust had been sorely misplaced.

Chapter 15

Exploring Anger, Impulsivity, Betrayal, and Truth

Enraged by the unraveling of his world, Norde's anger erupted into a violent outburst. His pent-up frustration and betrayal surged through him, leading him to physically confront Smith and demand Angelica's departure from the home he had mindlessly purchased for her.

The scene became chaotic as Smith lay wounded and unconscious on the floor, marked by Norde's explosion of anger. Angelica's cries for help pierced the air, calling attention to the tumultuous situation that had transpired behind closed doors. As the authorities rushed to the scene, Angelica promptly fabricated a tale of victimhood, presenting herself as an innocent bystander caught in a violent conflict.

When the authorities arrived, Angelica's narrative painted Norde as an intruder who had forcefully entered the house and attacked Smith, whom she conveniently referred to as her guest. As Angelica's version of events was unveiled, Norde found himself in the shocking position of being taken into custody. The swift turn of events had disrupted his life once more, thrusting him into a legal battle that would determine the course of his future.

As he awaited his hearing, Norde fought with the truth of his situation. The lines between truth and deception had become blurred. The severe contrast between the man he believed himself to be and the events that had transpired weighed profoundly on him.

Following Norde's hearing, the legal process came to a close with a combination of fines and probation, the results of his impulsive outburst. The effects had been acknowledged by the legal system, leading to a period of adaptation as he struggled with the aftermath.

As the dust settled and the probationary period began, Norde found himself constrained by the city that had once been his refuge. The stipulation that he couldn't leave Black River City for six months was a consequence of his anger.

Returning to his once-shared home, Norde was met with an eerie surprise. It didn't take long for him to discover that in his absence Angelica had sold the house, and moved away with the money. The house, which had once symbolized a secret connection, now stood as a major financial loss — a monument to the illusions that had crumbled before his eyes.

The solitude of those six months served as a period of reflection for Norde. The city that had once held the promise of excitement and newfound opportunities now felt like a cage. With each passing day, he was left to grapple with his mistakes and the search for a path forward, as he endured the chain of events set into motion.

Angelica's departure from Black River City leads her to a premeditated encounter with Hemeve. In an act motivated by anger, and a desire for retribution, Angelica approaches Hemeve at the auto shop in Parson's Town. With a heavy heart and a sense of revenge, she bears a burden that she believes must be shared. Her intention is clear — to unveil the truth and expose the secrets that had decayed in the shadows.

In the privacy of the auto shop, Angelica's manner is a grim contrast to the woman Norde had known. With vengeance and defiance, she hands over to Hemeve the set of intimate photographs, captured during the time she and Norde had first met in Black River. These images, taken in the heat of their passion, now serve as proof of their affair.

The images tell a story of betrayal, of Hemeve, and of the trust that had once existed between Norde and Angelica. With disregard, Angelica reveals the truth to Hemeve — the woman who had inadvertently become a collateral victim of their tangled emotions.

The act of revealing these private moments to Hemeve is a calculated move — an attempt to inflict pain and perhaps find a sense of vindication for the hurt she herself had experienced. Hemeve, taken surprised by the images before her, processes the situation with doubt and mistrust.

As Angelica's words weave the tale of her entanglement with Norde, Hemeve listens with sadness and frustration. The knowledge that Norde's actions had sparked a chain of events that reached its peak in this act of revenge leaves her struggling with the flip side of emotions. Hemeve, who had been in the dark about the affair, finds herself drawn into a narrative that shocked her. The knowledge that Norde is now incarcerated darkens the situation. The bond that had existed between Hemeve and Norde is now tainted by the betrayal and secrets that have come to light.

For Angelica, sharing the truth with Hemeve is a step towards revenge, an attempt to damage and shatter Norde's life. The photographs stand, leaving in their wake a trail of hurt and broken trust.

Filled with concern, confusion, and determination, Hemeve sets her sights on Black River. The journey is motivated by her need to uncover the truth, to confront Norde, and to salvage what remains of their relationship. As she arrives in Black River, her heart races with anticipation, yet she finds that what she faces is far more distressing than she could have imagined.

Despite her efforts to track him down, Norde remains a shadow, unreachable and untraceable. Hemeve's search leads her down a path of frustration, as she encounters dead ends and unanswered questions. Norde's absence is a silent barrier that prevents her from finding the closure she so desperately seeks.

Meanwhile, Norde's life in Black River is marked by confinement and filled with isolation. Restrained to leave the city due to his probation, he lives in a haunted exile. The fear of Angelica's threats lingers, making him apprehensive of any contact with Hemeve or the outside world. Months pass by, each day marked by uncertainty and the heavy hurdle of regret.

As Hemeve's search continues to yield no results, she is left to grapple with the absence of answers, frustration, sadness, and a growing sense of resignation. The story of Hemeve and Norde takes on a new dimension, defined by distance and silence, as they navigate the aftermath of his affair.

Chapter 16

Shattered Dreams: Norde's Solitude, Hemeve's Legacy

In the wake of the tumultuous events that transpired in Black River, Smith takes decisive action that further alters the course of Norde's life. Fueled by a sense of betrayal and a desire for revenge, Smith approaches the Brothers Alliance — the very organization Norde had become affiliated with. He paints Norde as a man of ill repute, highlighting the attack on Smith and the role he played in forcing Angelica out of town.

The Brothers Alliance's decision exerts a significant influence on his prospects and leaves him confronting an ambiguous future

With a depleted bank account, Norde's options are limited. He seeks refuge in an ordinary hotel, the remnants of his life now confined to a room and his thoughts. The isolation bears down on him. The once-promising trajectory of Norde's life has been irrevocably altered.

In the aftermath of his banishment, Norde is left to confront the future in solitude. The memories of his past are recalled through his present, as he struggles with the profound impact of decisions made under threat.

As Norde's life takes a downward spiral, the confines of the hotel room become a reflection of his turmoil. Stripped of his previous connections and opportunities, he finds himself ensnared in a cycle of solitude and bitterness. The isolation he experiences begins to burden greatly on his conscience, and the days blur into nights as the effects of his circumstances bear down on him.

The hotel room, once a temporary shelter, now serves as a metaphorical prison for Norde's emotions. Incapable to return to his former life in Parson, he becomes adrift, detached from any resemblance of routine or purpose. The bitterness that permeates his existence becomes a constant companion, seeping into every corner of his thoughts.

In an attempt to numb the pain and fill the void, Norde seeks refuge at the bar within the hotel building. It is there that he finds temporary relief in the company of fellow patrons and the embrace of alcohol. The line between day and night blurs, as he loses track of time and the boundaries that once governed his life. Drinking becomes a means of escape, a way to momentarily silence the memories of his past and the regrets that haunt him.

Trapped in a haze of intoxication, Norde's decisions become increasingly impulsive. One fateful night, after consuming a significant amount of alcohol, his intoxication led to an accident that landed him in the emergency house. The abrupt interruption to his self-destructive path shocks him out of his lethargy, if only temporarily. As he lies unconscious in the emergency house.

The accident that happened to Norde took a severe toll, leaving him with a concussion that plunged him into a deep and prolonged coma. As the days turned into weeks and the weeks into months, Norde remained unconscious, trapped in an intermediate state between wakefulness and oblivion. The accident's impact on his head had caused profound neurological trauma, rendering him unresponsive and removed from the world around him.

However, as the emergency house contacts Hemeve contending with the evolving situation, the medical forecast for Norde remains grim. While doing their utmost to provide care, the doctors held cautious expectations about his chances of regaining consciousness. They openly shared their doubts with Hemeve about the grim picture of his clinical condition. The uncertainty surrounding Norde's fate creates doubt over the possibility of his recovery, leaving Hemeve torn between expectation and the current circumstances.

The passage of time seemed to stretch endlessly, and the outside world moved forward while Norde's existence remained suspended in a perpetual slumber.

The momentum behind the installation of hydrants and the canalization of rivers persisted, sweeping through municipality after municipality like a transformative wave. Hydrants, symbols of progress and development, became a prevalent sight, adorning the streets and driveways of numerous residences. It was as though the landscape itself was evolving, adapting to the promise of a more efficient future.

Among this wave of change, Hemeve found herself called upon to play an even greater role in shaping the transportation landscape. Invited to take on a significant public position, she accepted the role of secretary of transportation for her county. The responsibility rested on her shoulders as she embraced the challenges and opportunities that came with this new position. Her expertise and forward-thinking vision positioned her as a key figure in the ongoing revolution of public transportation.

With her two sons as steadfast allies, Hemeve set out to further revolutionize the way people moved within and between communities. The interurban hydroelectric trams she introduced marked a new episode in the transportation saga. The hydro trams connected towns and cities, bridging gaps and growing a sense of collaboration that extended beyond geographical boundaries. The power of hydro technology, harnessed by Hemeve's invention, was once again at the forefront of public progress.

Chapter 17

Interwoven Destinies: Embracing Winter's Revolution

As winter settled in, casting its frosty spell, a new phase began in the lives of those who had been connected. The passage of three years had brought about unforeseen changes, and the threads of time continued to weave patterns.

Tragedy struck the household of Smith, a man whose path had been both connected and divergent from Norde's. The chilling hold of tuberculosis claimed the life of Smith's wife, leaving behind a cold void. The bond between Smith and his daughter, Jamela, tightened as they navigated the world as a now-grieving family. The warmth of a mother's presence had been replaced by an ache, and their lives shifted as they learned to embrace a new circumstance.

During this emotional period, Smith found himself stepping into a new role. The once steadfast owner of the general store, he now found himself accompanying Hemeve on her journeys as secretary of transportation.

Meanwhile, the younger generation took their places at the forefront of the general store. Togora and Jamela, resilient and adaptable, stepped into the shoes that their parents had once occupied. Their youthful vigor injected new life into the store, breathing fresh energy into its corridors. As Togora and Jamela navigated the business, their journey reflected the broader narrative of evolution and growth that marked the lives of those in Parson's Town.

In this fabric of interconnected lives, the winds of change continued to blow. The threads of time, once apparently isolated, converged and diverged. The landscape transformed, new characters stepped onto the stage, and the legacy of discovery and progress continued to shape the course of history.

As the pages of time turned, the industrious minds of Cypress and Dusk pressed forward with their pioneering work in the field of electrochemistry. Their dedication to refining and enhancing electrolytic batteries became an everlasting journey of discovery, with each step yielding remarkable progress.

Their pursuit of efficiency led them to explore original techniques in the processing and manipulation of the clay solution that served as the foundation of their battery cells. Through dedicated experimentation, they discovered methods that increased the cells' power many times over. Their mastery over the nuances of the clay solution's composition and behavior unlocked newfound potential, propelling their work to new heights.

Although, their journey extended beyond conventional paths, Cypress and Dusk, dared to venture into untraveled territories. With audacious curiosity, they turned their attention to the world of precious metals, harnessing the capabilities of silver, gold, and other rare elements to create electrode rods. These new components introduced a layer of sophistication to their creations, enhancing the cells' capabilities in remarkable ways.

The duo's expertise was vast, leading them to explore materials as original as volcanic ash. This apparently unconventional choice turned out to be a stroke of brilliance, as the original properties of volcanic ash enriched their clay fluid with unprecedented qualities. Their combination of natural elements and scientific aptitude went far beyond the borders of Parson's Town.

As Cypress and Dusk delved deeper into their research, they became beacons of creativity, their laboratory a place of transformation. Their work spread across the landscape, weaving a tale of dedication, experimentation, and breakthroughs. With each stride forward, they inched closer to reshaping the sphere of electrolytic batteries, an achievement that would ripple through history's pages for generations.

In the gentle embrace of a spring morning, Norde's eyes flickered open after a nearly six-year slumber in the depths of a coma. His awakening was a fragile transition as if he were a wraith emerging from the shadows of a dreamlike world. The passage of time had produced a profound transformation upon his once vibrant form, leaving behind a hollow visage that displayed little resemblance to the man he once was.

His voice, once lively and vibrant, now emerged as a whisper, as though it carried the weight of the years he had spent in his silent repose. His lean figure, stripped of the vitality that had once defined him, seemed like a mere shadow of its former self. Deep-set eyes peered out from expansive sockets, and cheeks seemed to have sunk inwards, revealing his features in an otherworldly pallor.

Weeks stretched before him as Norde embarked on a slow and arduous journey toward recovery. Within the confines of his room at the emergency house, he began to gradually regain his strength. The passage of each day marked incremental steps towards his restoration, a process that represented the gentle bloom of spring itself. As the world outside his window burst forth in vibrant colors and renewed life, Norde's own reawakening expanded in sync with nature's flow.

As Norde's body gained back its vitality and his voice regained its strength, he found himself walking a path of change that reflected the seasons. Just as spring's gentle touch encourages life from the earth, Norde's awakening breathed new life into his existence, allowing him to emerge from the depths of darkness into the embrace of a world renewed.

Gently, the nurse at the emergency house shared with Norde the details of his circumstances, as he listened with surprise and uncertainty. The fog of his memories began to lift, revealing the remnants of the accident and the years that had slipped away from him. It was a strange realization that nearly six years had passed since that fateful day.

As the nurse spoke, Norde's mind flickered with recollections of his past, each memory forming a thread in the fabric of his life that he had been unconsciously weaving during his long slumber. The world he remembered seemed foreign, a place that had carried on without him. The nurse's words echoed in his mind, confirming the passage of time that he had missed.

He learned that Hemeve had been reached out to and approached as his emergency contact, and she had responded by making yearly payments for his care at the emergency house. However, the nurse revealed that

Hemeve hadn't visited since that initial contact. This knowledge struck a chord within Norde. He felt longing and regret, sensing that the threads connecting him to his past had faded over the years.

Feeling a perplexing rush of emotions, Norde made a decision. He asked the nurse to refrain from contacting Hemeve, to keep their current situation a secret from her. The nurse, understanding his request, agreed to respect his wishes. At that moment, Norde fought with the implications of his choice – to continue his journey of recovery without the presence of the woman he had once shared his life with.

As the days went by, Norde found himself navigating a landscape that was unknown. His physical strength was gradually returning, while his emotions were still a vast terrain to explore. With each step forward, he confronted the memories of the past and the uncertainties of the future.

PART V

Chapter 18

Rediscovering Life: Norde's Reflections and Rebirth

As days turned into weeks, Norde found himself settling into a routine within the walls of the emergency house. The once-unfamiliar environment gradually became his new life, and the care he received nourished his body and spirit. The nurturing meals and genuine attention from the staff acted as stepping stones on his journey toward a more active life.

Norde's strength returned with surprising speed, reflecting his own resilience and the restorative atmosphere of the emergency house. He embraced the routines of daily life, shedding the confinement of his room and embracing the shared spaces of the house. No longer confined to his bed, he began to use it only for its intended purpose – a place for restful sleep.

Norde transitioned to having his meals in the collective dining room, marking his integration into the life of the emergency house. The simple act of sharing meals with fellow patients, engaging in conversations, and being surrounded by a community brought a sense of normalcy that had eluded him during his long coma.

In addition to his physical progress, Norde started to explore his emotional landscape. Memories, feelings, and reflections flooded his thoughts, often prompting him to contemplate the path that led him to this point. As he regained his strength, he also gained clarity and perspective.

With each step he took and each connection he made, Norde was redefining his identity and forging a new sense of purpose. The journey of recovery was about healing his body and rediscovering his place in the world and the people who remained a part of his life, even if from a distance. As he navigated his way forward, Norde found himself drawn to the idea that the future held opportunities for growth, renewal, and a chance to mend the threads that had worn out over time.

As Norde's days and nights continued within the walls of the emergency house, his mind became a labyrinth of memories, regrets, and contemplations. The passage of time had turned into a reflection of his life – moments that stretched from the vibrant days of his work as the town's procurement officer.

Hemeve's face, once a source of warmth and comfort, now haunted his thoughts. He replayed the scenes of their life together, the joy they shared, and the plans they once had. The longing to see his children's smiles and hear their laughter sounded through his mind.

The transformation of Parson and the countryside farm weighed significantly on him. He remembered the joy he felt watching Hemeve's talent bring prosperity to their lives, the water wheel and pump becoming symbols of his family's achievements. While reminiscing, bitterness arose as he traced the threads that connected Smith's actions to his downfall.

The truth, laid bare by Angelica, had exposed a web of deceit orchestrated by Smith and manipulated by the Brothers Alliance. The resentment that simmered within Norde grew more potent with every recollection. He feels like a pawn in a larger game, his life torn apart by the schemes of others.

In the confines of his room at the emergency house, Norde's emotions roiled like a tempestuous sea. He wrestled with his anger and sense of betrayal while recognizing that his own choices had played a role in his downfall. But the knowledge that he had been manipulated, that he had fallen into a trap set by those he once considered friends, fueled the fire of his resentment.

Leaving behind the boundaries of the emergency house, Norde stepped into a world that felt foreign and familiar. The air was crisp and carried the promise of new beginnings, a rigid contrast to the shadows he had lived in for years. As he made his way to the bank of Black River, he felt a combination of trepidation and determination.

Walking through the bank's doors, Norde approached the teller and requested to access his account. The anticipation weighed deeply on him, but when he received the news that his account still held a balance, relief washed over him. It was an encouragement, a resource that could help him piece together the parts of his life that had shattered.

With a renewed sense of purpose, Norde made his way to the hotel where he had stayed before. The surroundings seemed different now – a place that had seen his journey, a witness to the storm he had weathered. As he settled into his room, he began to sketch out his plans. His first step was to reconnect with Hemeve, to bridge the gap that had grown between them.

Hemeve's memory lingered in his mind. He knew that facing her would require courage, honesty, and a willingness to lay bare his mistakes. He yearned to reclaim the life he had lost, to rekindle the flame of their bond, and to make amends for the wrongs he had committed.

Walking through the streets of Black River, Norde found himself immersed in a scene that was familiar and foreign at the same time. The energetic activity of hydro vehicles moving along the streets caught his attention, each one outfitted with the same faceplates and connectors that Hemeve had cleverly designed for their own hydro cart. It was as if her invention had taken root and flourished into a widespread revolution in transportation.

As he watched the hydro vehicles gliding gracefully along the roads, memories of their own hydro cart came rushing back to him – the excitement of those early days, the joy of riding together, and the sense of pioneering a new mode of transportation. But now, this invention had expanded far beyond their own experiences, becoming an integral part of everyday life for the people of Black River.

Norde's heart filled up with joy and nostalgia. He felt a sense of connection to the progress that had been made, knowing that Hemeve's vision had played a significant role in shaping the current landscape. The hydrants installed in front of every residence represented her legacy and the positive impact she had made in the world.

In the middle of the busy streets and the storm of changes, Norde found a glimmer of hope. Perhaps, he thought, the same spirit of progress could find its way into his own life. With renewed determination, he continued his journey, eager to reconnect with Hemeve and find his own place in the evolving world around him.

Chapter 19

Emotional Turmoil: Confronting Revenge, Finding Closure

Norde's determination to win back Hemeve's affection and trust drove him to focus on his appearance and strive for a fresh start. With a clear goal in mind, he set a date in the near future to reunite with her and show how he had changed during his time away.

As the date of their reunion approached, Norde was filled with excitement and apprehension. He was eager to reveal the transformation he had undergone during his time away – both physically and emotionally. He knew that this encounter could be his last chance to mend their damaged relationship and reclaim the life they had once shared.

He was prepared to lay bare his feelings, his regrets, and his determination to make amends. He had hoped that their reunion would mark a new beginning, a chance to rebuild the bond they had lost.

In the days leading up to the date Norde had chosen to approach Hemeve, his emotions were sent into a spiral of shock, hurt, and a burning desire for revenge by the sight of a newspaper article during his breakfast. As he stared at the seemingly perfect family portrait, his thoughts and emotions raged within him. The article portrayed Hemeve and Smith as the inventive and industrious couple responsible for pioneering the transportation revolution that had swept through towns and cities, both near and far.

Unaware to Norde, Hemeve had accepted Smith's marriage proposal after enduring years of heartache, uncertainty, and solitude brought on by his absence. The betrayal she felt due to Norde's affair with Angelica had caused irreparable damage to their relationship. The news article's failure to acknowledge Norde's role in Hemeve's life and the misattribution of his own sons as Smith's children felt like a deliberate erasure of his existence, intensifying the pain of the years spent away from his family.

Norde's simmering anger toward Smith, fueled by his past betrayals, reached a boiling point. The desire for revenge consumed him, growing hotter with each passing moment. He felt an overwhelming urge to make Smith pay for what he perceived as the theft of his life – his wife, his children, and the recognition he deserved. Norde's once-peaceful breakfast table had turned into a battleground of emotions, with the single thought of vengeance a constant presence in his mind.

As Norde walked through the dimly lit streets, his heart pounded with anger, anxiety, and fear. His mind was consumed by thoughts of revenge, convinced that ending Smith's life was the only way to regain his sense of vindication and justice.

The streets of the underground market were a harsh contrast to the world Norde once knew. The shadows seemed to replicate the darkness he felt within himself. He navigated through a maze of alleyways until he found the dealer he had heard about. In exchange for the money he had withdrawn from the bank, Norde obtained a weapon – something that could potentially carry out the act he believed would bring him closure.

With the weapon hidden away, Norde's steps quickened, his mind racing with the ramifications of his decision. The struggle intensified. While revenge seemed like the answer, deep down, he knew the path he was on was wrong. Memories of his life before the accident, the love he once shared with Hemeve, and the family he had started all tugged at his conscience.

As he stood outside the hotel, the gravity of his plan hit him with full force. He remembered the faces of his children, the innocence he saw in their eyes, and the bond they shared. Norde's hands trembled as he gripped the weapon, torn between the desire for revenge and the lingering pieces of his former self that yearned for mending and repair.

As Norde arrived at the hydro tram station, he was confronted once again by the public recognition of Hemeve's accomplishments. The plaques and honors seemed to add to his own sense of bitterness and loss. As he waited for the last tram to Parson, his thoughts were a tempest of anger, jealousy, and his ever-present desire for revenge.

The journey on the hydro tram felt otherworldly to Norde. The new city lights, also powered by hydro technology, and the passing scenery blurred in his mind as his thoughts raced through his plans. Arriving in Parson, he found himself drawn to the vicinity of Smith's general store, his heart pounding with tension and anxiety.

The night was long and restless. Norde lurked in the shadows, fighting with the repercussions of his decision. The gun he had acquired felt heavy in his pocket. He replayed memories of his past with Hemeve, the love they once shared, and the family they had built together. The pain of his betrayal and the subsequent events consumed him, but so did the desire for retribution.

As the night turned into dawn, Norde's exhaustion grew. The first rays of sunlight lightened the streets, radiating a soft glow over the surroundings. It was in this moment, between darkness and dawn, that Norde had to make a choice that would determine the course of his future.

The gun pressed against his leg, the choice he held in his hands. As he gazed at Smith's general store, Norde's anger seemed to waver. He remembered the faces of his sons, the happiness he once felt, and the love he had for Hemeve. The desire for revenge was still present, but so was the realization that taking Smith's life would reinforce the pain he had endured.

Chapter 20

Tragic Morning: Unfolding Chaos, Shattered Lives

As Smith opened the doors of the general store, Norde's finger squeezed the trigger, the loud bang shattered the morning stillness. The gunshots echoed through the quiet air, piercing the tranquility of the town. Norde fired twice in Smith's direction.

The first bullet missed its target, flying past Smith and embedding itself into the wall of a nearby building. Smith, startled and caught off guard, stumbled for cover. Norde watched as Smith reached for safety, as he recognizes the gravity of what he had done.

Panic and confusion swept over the scene as the sound of the gunshots reached the ears of nearby residents. Moments later, the street was filled with commotion. People rushed to the scene, calling for help and shouting in alarm.

Norde's pulse quickened as he saw the panic he had caused, and his mind was flooded with regret, fear, and a profound sense of guilt. Shouts in the distance, grow louder with each passing moment.

The second bullet found its mark, striking Hemeve as she stepped out of the store just behind Smith. A muffled gasp escaped her lips as the impact knocked her back, her hand instinctively seizing her bleeding shoulder.

At the sound of the gunshot and Hemeve's cry, Jamela's voice struck the air with a scream that mirrored her shock and terror. She emerged from the store, eyes wide with panic, her face quickly turning pale as she saw her mother-in-law bleeding on the ground. The street seemed to fade away as panic surged through her veins.

Hemeve's strength faltered, and she stumbled towards the hydrant, leaving a trail of blood behind her. Her eyes locked onto Norde, with pain, confusion, and accusation. The world around her seemed to recede as the gravity of the situation weighed down on her.

The scene was a portrait of tragedy – Hemeve wounded and struggling to stay conscious, Jamela's horrified screams, and Norde standing in the aftermath of his impulsive actions. The air was heavy with shock and sorrow, the strain of the situation suffocating.

As the blasts of the gunshots faded, the commotion continued, with sounds of the town in distress.

Togora's arrival at the scene added another layer of heartbreak to the developing tragedy. His eyes widened in shock as he took in the sight of his wounded mother lying on the ground. Ignoring the commotion around him, he rushed to her side, his hands trembling as he tried to halt the bleeding and offer her some comfort.

Meanwhile, Norde, now recognizing the full extent of the catastrophe he had caused, turned to flee the scene. His heart raced, his mind a storm panic and fear. He looked at the gun in his hand, the tool of his misguided intentions, and then at the chaos emerging around him. It was a harsh path he had been on – a path that had brought him to the brink of destruction. The trouble of his anger and his thirst for revenge were all too heavy to bear. But before he could take more than a few steps, an iron pipe descended upon his head with a sickening bang. The blow, delivered by the enraged owner of the nearby establishment who had witnessed the entire tragic sequence of events, knocked Norde to the ground, rendering him unconscious.

The bystanders who had gathered on the street were frozen in shock, incapable of fully processing the rapid sequence of events. The air was heavy with a sense of sorrow, the gravity of the situation settling over the scene like a heavy fog.

As Togora looked at his unconscious father lying on the ground, a surge of emotions swept over him. Conflicting feelings of anger, confusion, and sadness mingled within him. The sight was heart-wrenching, leaving him struggling with the violence of the events.

Inside the store, Hemeve was rushed to a more stable location, where she was carefully tended to by Jamela. With her daughter-in-law's help, she managed to stop the bleeding and stabilize her condition to some extent. The doctor who lived nearby quickly arrived on the scene upon hearing the cries for help, and he began to provide the medical attention that Hemeve urgently needed.

In the chaos, the town's Sheriff arrived, evaluating the situation and taking charge of the scene. Norde, still unconscious, was taken into custody once again.

As the town came to terms with the tragic events that had occurred, Smith unharmed, collaborated with the authorities at the scene.

The following morning, a somber atmosphere settled over Parson's town. Friends, family, and community members gathered to offer their support to a woman whose life had been merged with the town's history.

Meanwhile, Norde remained in custody, transferred to the jail in Black River where he awaited his judgment. He was now the focal point of legal proceedings, as the town sought to grapple with the aftermath of the violence that had shattered its peace.

Chapter 21

NIGHT'S BETRAYAL:
CONFRONTING REGRET,
UNANSWERED LOSS

As Norde sat in his jail cell, contending with the enormity of the tragedy he had played a role in, he came across a newspaper article that painted a vivid picture of the events that had transpired. The headline "Secretary of Transportation Survives Deadly Attack" immediately caught his attention, and he began to read the details of the story that had spread out.

The article recounted the shooting incident, highlighting how Hemeve, the inventive and influential figure in the transportation industry, had narrowly escaped a grave fate. The story spoke of her daughter-in-law's quick response and the intervention of the town doctor, both of whom had played a significant role in saving Hemeve's life.

Reading the words on the newspaper page, Norde was struck by the realization of the irreparable damage he had caused. He had endangered the life of someone he had once cared deeply for. The guilt and remorse settled upon him.

During his contemplation, Norde began to reflect on the journey that had led him to this point. The choices, betrayals, and misunderstandings that had happened over the years had reached a tragic event that had left a trail of blood and sorrow in its wake. As he read the article, he wondered if there could have been a different path, a way to mend what had been broken and to find a better resolution to the conflicts that had plagued his life.

Sitting alone in his jail cell, Norde wrestled with the profound emotions that had brought him to this point. The words on the newspaper page prompted him to confront the depths of his regret and the realization that there could be no turning back from the course that had been set in motion.

In the dead of night, as the town slumbered under the cover of darkness, a fateful encounter awaited Norde. The sheriff from Black River City arrived at Norde's jail cell, accompanied by a guard, and delivered a surprising message – he was to be released from custody. Perplexed and in doubt, Norde stepped out of his cell, his mind racing with confusion.

As he emerged onto the streets, disorientation clouded Norde's thoughts. He began to wander adrift, his steps guided by an instinctive need to put distance between himself and the jail that had confined him. In the shadows of a dark corner, he encountered a group of men, their faces hidden in the obscurity of the night. One among them was a familiar face – a member of the Brothers Alliance, a connection to his past that he was apprehended to.

The man's presence ignited a glimmer of hope within Norde – a belief that perhaps his release was guided by those who once held influence over his life. Gratitude and relief grew within him as he voiced his appreciation for his sudden liberation. But the response he received was unexpected and chilling – he was told to flee, to vanish into the night.

Complying with their directive, Norde started to move away, walking deeper into the darkness of the alley, his footsteps carrying him away from the group. Yet, before he could comprehend the gravity of the situation, a hail of gunshots burst forth from behind him. The shadows seemed to come alive with the sound of the shots, and Norde's body was struck multiple times.

As the barrage of gunfire ceased, Norde's inert form crumpled to the ground, his fate sealed in a tragic and brutal manner. The darkness of the night testifies to the completion of a tumultuous journey, as Norde's story comes to a violent and abrupt end.

The morning sun shed its light upon the town, and the front page of the newspaper carried a headline that sent shockwaves through the community: "Sheriff's Officer Shoots Dead Runaway Prisoner". As the townspeople went about their day, reading the article, one person's heart sank with a heavy sense of recognition and sorrow. Hemeve, reading the paper, immediately saw Norde's name imprinted in the desolate black and white print, and a profound sense of lamentation washed over her.

At that moment, Hemeve's mind was filled with a disarray of emotions – grief, confusion, and a deep sense of loss. She knew that the man who had once held a special place in her life was now gone, and with him, many unanswered questions remained. The results of the tragedy that had taken place left her struggling with the enormity of the situation.

Hemeve had lost Norde, an individual who had played a significant role in her life, in circumstances that were cloaked in secrecy and obscurity. The truth behind Norde's actions, the motivations that drove him to try to take another man's life, were now buried with him. As Hemeve absorbed the news, a sense of sadness and helplessness settled upon her – the knowledge that some things would forever remain obscure, and that closure might forever elude her.

In the middle of a town that continued to buzz with life, Hemeve carried a heavy burden of grief and the pressure of the past. The entanglements of the human experience, the choices that shape destinies, and the crimes that sometimes remain unsolved were all encapsulated in the tragic tale that had spread out. As the day pressed on, the people of the town moved forward, each carrying their own memories and questions, while Hemeve silently mourned the end of a significant part of her life.

Appendix

This appendix invites you to explore additional visual content and resources related to the themes discussed in the book "Hydrant For Electric Vehicles." To access a collection of historic electric vehicle photos, clarifying animations, a downloadable 3D model of an actual hydrant for an electric vehicle, and shop for souvenirs, visit www.h4ev.cc.

By visiting the website, you'll find:

- Photo Albums: View images showcasing historic electric vehicles, illustrating the evolution of early electric transportation.

- Animation: Explore an animated presentation showcasing the inner workings of the hydrant for electric vehicles and the charging process. This captivating animation provides an in-depth understanding of how the technology works.

- 3D Model: Download and experience a 3D model that vividly demonstrates the mechanics of a hydrant for electric vehicles. This interactive model offers a hands-on visualization of the technology described in the book.

Visit www.h4ev.cc to access these valuable resources. Note that some content may require a 3D printer and assembly. All material is for educational purposes.

Thank you for exploring the themes and concepts within "Hydrant For Electric Vehicles." We hope these visual resources enhance your understanding and appreciation of the book's themes and concepts.